I0590922

Blowback

A "Cadillac" Holland Mystery

H. Max Hiller

Copyright © 2017 by H. Max Hiller

Second Edition published April 2020
By Indies United Publishing House, LLC

All rights reserved worldwide. No part of this publication may be replicated, redistributed, or given away in any form without the prior written consent of the author/publisher or the terms relayed to you herein.

ISBN: 978-1-64456-114-0
Library of Congress Control Number: 2020934712

INDIES UNITED PUBLISHING HOUSE, LLC
P.O. BOX 3071
QUINCY, IL 62305-3071

www.indiesunited.net

Cover Image by the Author

Hurricane Katrina produced a number of humorous examples of unexpected imagery. This striking image perfectly illustrates the novel's theme of unintended consequences. The city was as badly battered by the recovery efforts as it had been by the storm, but the one thing that never wavered was the city's sense of humor about things like this.

To Bill and Emily and the road not taken.

1

I HAVE ANSWERED to a number of things: nicknames, military ranks, and more or less profane epithets in my thirty-eight years. I have preferred each and every one of them to the name Cooter Holland, which my father bestowed upon me at birth in honor of his hometown in the boot-heel of Missouri. The stories most people tell as to how they washed up in New Orleans in the wake of Hurricane Katrina are generally self-serving lies. I was born and raised here, but the story of my return after nearly two decades away begins with a shady intelligence operation that went horribly awry in Baghdad. It's a story I won't be sharing here.

The mission ended in an ambush that nearly took my life. My parents were misinformed that I was presumed dead, and that my body had not been recovered. The error was not corrected for nearly six months. I spent twenty months rebuilding myself physically and mentally from the injuries I suffered in the attack before I used my family's political connections to join the Louisiana State Patrol as a Level 2 Inspector with an indefinite appointment to New Orleans under the watchful eye of NOPD's Chief of Detectives. Chief Avery had been my father's patrol partner before they both made detective, and

Avery had assumed the leadership role vacated by my father's retirement. Chief Avery understood my true motivation in joining the state patrol had nothing to do with preserving law and order. I wanted to have access to their resources to solve the mystery of my father's disappearance while conducting boat rescue operations in the Lower Ninth Ward after Hurricane Katrina.

The Italian-Iraqi operative who saved my life in the Baghdad ambush had recently immigrated to New Orleans, using the name Tony Vento, to open the sort of Italian bistro he had long dreamed about owning. My kid-sister had handled the EB-5 visa for Tony. She also seemed to be ignoring my strongly worded instructions that she maintain a strictly professional relationship with the admittedly good-looking foreigner. I could not explain my position without divulging the true connection between Tony and I or sharing graphic details about his knife skills and his comfort level with violence.

I say all of this to explain how I came to be sitting at the end of the bar in the St. Charles Tavern on the Saturday before St. Patrick's Day two years after Hurricane Katrina. The Tavern, as its regulars refer to it, dates to the era when this stretch of St. Charles Avenue was lined with dive bars servicing the stevedores and the surrounding working-class neighborhood. It was owned by Silver Dollar Carollo, the mobster who preceded Carlos Marcello as the godfather of New Orleans organized crime. Carollo supplemented the tavern's income by running hookers on the second floor. The Tavern was where my father would scold me over breakfast after gathering me up from a holding cell at the Second

District every time that I was caught drinking under age in the Quarter.

It had served generations of locals and tourists as a pre-dawn source of greasy food to stop stomachs full of alcohol for Tulane students and a last meal of the day for Uptown residents on their way home from nights out on the town, but the place was struggling to rebuild its brand in post-Katrina New Orleans. The influx of people who came to rebuild the city seemed to have little interest in the culinary landmarks of their newly adopted city. They publicly praised New Orleans' culture but privately despised the way the city equated run-down with history.

I was waiting on Chief Avery to arrive for our morning debriefing, so I made small talk with the rowdy Hibernian Parade marshals convened at the largest table for their annual free breakfast and cocktails before leading their St. Patrick's parade, which is always held on the Saturday before the holiday to ensure a larger crowd. The quality of our conversation deteriorated as the Jameson's portion of their annual breakfast took effect.

I excused myself when Chief Avery came through the door with a group of Sixth District officers. The Tavern became Avery's unofficial office after he followed Miss J here when she couldn't afford to reopen the diner she had operated with her sister, Esther, in the Lower Ninth Ward until the floodwall broke. Miss J's first cooking job was at a pre-school breakfast program the Black Panthers ran in the Florida Projects when my father was just a rookie cop.

Avery was already in the middle of a long day, which had started about three o'clock that Saturday morning with a shooting only ten blocks away. He arrived wearing the disgruntled look of just about every commander I had ever served under. Avery is taller than me, and he is wider at both his chest and his belt line. He has a head of graying black hair and the accent of someone born and raised in the Gentilly neighborhood. His wife broke him of buying off-the-rack suits from one of those places you can get a suit with two pairs of pants and a tie for one low price when he moved up the command ladder. His suits are now from Rothschild's on Canal and fit his build just right, but he still sweats right through a couple of shirts a day, no matter the season. I was, by contrast, in jeans and a hooded pullover bearing the State Police logo to conceal the body armor I wore. It was as close to a uniform as I ever wore anymore. I had spent my last years in the Army with a Tier-One unit whose members never wore a military uniform or displayed the rank of any of its members. That habit was hard to break, and Chief Avery had not told me to dress otherwise.

I was in better condition than my boss because I exercised every day as physical rehabilitation for the gunshot wounds in my shoulder and double kneecap replacement. Avery tolerated my hair being shaggier than regulation because it hid the surgical scars from where a number of titanium plates were used to rebuild my skull, which was shattered in the ambush. I was still getting used to the handsome new face my sister picked out of a magazine because she had no pictures of me when it was time for the facial reconstructive surgeries. Her choice provided NOPD officers with their first derisive nickname for me: 'Hollywood.'

"What's up?" I asked as Avery pulled a wooden chair across the mosaic tile floor and motioned for me to join him at his favorite table by the front window.

"You know that lecture that you always give the detectives I partner you with, the one about unintended consequences?" Avery began.

"I call it blowback. What about it?"

"Suffice it to say that the blowback of your actions last night means we need to come up with a Plan B," he said. This was a conversation we both knew was coming for a while. I was not a good fit for his department and neither his own detectives nor I were even trying to make things work any longer. "You have managed to wear out your welcome with the National Guard after that chase you talked them into last night. You're too politically connected for me fire you, which was Plan A, but there's obviously no point in assigning you any more training partners."

"You do remember what my father used to say about making plans, don't you? Everything works out but nothing works out the way you planned." I knew that Avery could not afford to lose my bothersome help because NOPD was still running at less than eighty percent of its authorized strength dur to the number of officers who had left since the storm. "For the record, we caught the guys we were chasing last night."

"But you used National Guard soldiers carrying unloaded weapons to form a roadblock that could have easily become a shootout. Their commander has ordered you out of the Ninth Ward," Avery elaborated on his predicament.

Avery was being nice about this. I had been repeatedly ordered to let the National Guard be the ones to patrol the city's least-recovered post-storm neighborhood. Less than fifty percent of the city's evacuated population had returned, but the Lower Ninth Ward had fewer than ten percent of its pre-storm population. Returning homeowners were enduring unreliable water and electrical services and almost non-existent medical, police, and mass transportation services just to live in the only place they had ever called home.

I was irresistibly drawn to the area because it felt so much like the part of Baghdad where I ran my last operation. Avery, and the detectives he had assigned me in the two months I had been under his command, saw no practical value in my nocturnal patrols of the unlit streets. He preferred to believe they were part of my ongoing search for information on my father's disappearance in the area rather than a symptom of the hyper-awareness form of PTSD that the state police psychiatrists had warned him I suffered from.

Our conversation was interrupted by the server offering us menus. Avery waved the menus away and ordered omelets stuffed with crawfish etouffee for both of us. It wasn't what I would have selected, but I knew it was a good choice. They would arrive with a mound of grilled potatoes and onions and fresh-baked biscuits. Avery ordered coffee. I asked for an RC Cola, this being the only place in town still selling my favorite childhood soda.

"So, what do you have in mind?" I prodded Avery to finish latest unofficial admonishment.

"I still need to justify your salary to FEMA, and I need to find something for you to do that I don't want to assign to the few detectives I have. The parts of your military record that aren't redacted mention you were involved in tracking down bad guys," Avery said in a tone intended to get me to elaborate. I had nothing to share with him.

"Worse guys than you have," was all I said. I was comfortable assuming Avery was not going to allow me the same kill-or-capture option I had overseas. I had been part of a unit that tracked down Al Qaeda, ISIS, and Taliban leaders in places far less friendly or secure than New Orleans. The job did not involve politely knocking on doors and asking if they were home. I was worried that Avery intended to relegate me to some sort of make-work meant to make me quit my job.

"I need you to look for a suspect in a shooting who's been trying to intimidate the primary witnesses against him," Avery informed me.

"Why can't your guys handle this?" The situation sounded serious enough to justify that his own detectives handle it.

"Time is an issue. Michael Ferris was released on his own recognizance and then his attorney reported he was missing when the DA asked him to bring his client in for questioning about the gun he used in the shooting," Avery began to explain the case's finer details. "Three men attacked Ferris in a club in the French Quarter. He killed two of them, but the last one escaped. We found a blood trail and think he may have been hit as well. The DA was inclined to dismiss the shooting as an act of self-defense until the ATF ran the serial numbers on the guns involved. It turns out that the pistol Ferris used to defend himself and the guns on the men he shot were all stolen from a gun shop in Laramie, Wyoming over a year ago."

"You said finding him is time sensitive." I sensed that the task Avery was handing me had almost nothing to do with the shooting or the stolen guns. involved. Something else sent him in my direction. "What's really going on?"

"The shooting took place in a nightclub owned by Janelle Beauvoir and her husband."

"The singer?" I had seen Janelle perform at a number of benefits since I had come home. She was active in raising money to help the hundreds of musicians displaced by the storm who were still trying to come back to New Orleans.

"Ferris has threatened to kill her if she and her husband don't recant their statements. She's singing the first set at French Quarter Fest, which means you have something like a month to find the guy. She won't go on stage if he's still running around loose." Now I saw Avery's problem. NOPD definitely lacked the manpower to organize a full-scale manhunt while providing the Beauvoirs with 24/7 witness protection. It would also look far worse for Avery than the District Attorney if Janelle Beauvoir was murdered before a live audience. "The best NOPD can hope is to catch the guy in a traffic stop."

"Fine, I'll track him down, but what else aren't you telling me?" I knew Avery's body language too well to believe all I had to do was find his fugitive.

"The guys that got shot were members of some outfit in Texas called the Grassy Knoll Gun Club. The ATF has been after them for a few years for gun sales to whacko militias and survivalist groups. They have linked the ballistics on the pistol Ferris used to defend himself to some gang-related shootings here. Everyone wants to know how a gun from Wyoming wound up being used in gang shootings we cannot tie to one, and then into the hands of a guy we cannot link to those shootings or to the Texans he shot." Chief Avery was obviously confounded by the particulars of the case. He also seemed very relieved to have dumped the responsibility for sorting things out on the State Police. "One other thing for you to keep in mind is that Janelle's nightclub is the mayor's new favorite place to hang out in the Quarter, so getting this guy off their back will be a nice IOU with the Mayor down the line."

The mayor was in his last term, but I was in no position to refuse Chief Avery. I chewed my breakfast while Avery chatted with the uniformed officers from the Sixth District. He picked their brains for anything they knew about the dead guy in the latest shooting, and then inquired about how many additional homeowners, and how many known criminals, had returned to the neighborhood since the last time he took the Sixth District's pulse. Very few property owners in the neighborhood could afford flood insurance, so rebuilding the core of the city was going to take longer than surrounding neighborhoods. The patrol officers also voiced their concern about the increased number of muggings of undocumented Hispanics who had come to town to do storm cleanup and stayed on to do roofing and drywall work. They said the local gangs were calling them 'walking ATMs' because these workers were paid in cash but couldn't open bank accounts.

"One other thing," Avery said with a grin as we finished breakfast. "All I want you to do is to track the guy down. Just let me know where he is. I'll send NOPD detectives to make the arrest."

"So the State Police gets the blame if I fail and NOPD gets the collar if I succeed. That's a win-win for you either way."

"And you thought I didn't understand what

unintended consequences are." The Chief laughed at his comment harder than I did.

He motioned for me to follow him out of the Tavern and led me around the corner of the building to the parking lot. "Your room at the Holiday Inn is done now that you are persona non grata with the National Guard. That means you are going to need a car of your own to get around in."

Avery handed me the keys to the black Cadillac CTS he had been driving. NOPD's entire fleet of vehicles had been destroyed patrolling the brackish floodwaters that had covered eighty percent of New Orleans, so the department had commandeered the inventory of the city's only Cadillac dealership, and this was one of the last of those cars still in use.

Avery pointed to the files he left for me on the passenger seat with the pertinent details about the man I needed to find and the family I was now expected to protect. "Meet me at the Beauvoir's club on Decatur Street at six tonight. Wear something nice."

"I guess we'll have to change your name, Hollywood," the uniformed NOPD sergeant who followed us out of the Tavern joked as he leaned through the black sedan's open window.

"What do you have in mind?"

"I think we'll start calling you 'Cadillac.' It suits a rich kid like you better anyway." I let him have his fun without taking as much offense as he intended.

Like I said, I have preferred every name I have ever been given over the one my father gave me.

2

M Y FATHER INFLICTED my younger sister with the name Tulip, which says all you need to know about his sense of humor. We were raised in a four-bedroom ranch-style house near the Seventeenth Street Canal in the city's Lakefront neighborhood near the restaurants of the West End. Our home was damaged beyond repair when the canal's floodwalls collapsed under the stress of Katrina's wind-driven storm surge. My father had built a weekend place on the old highway to Biloxi when I was still a child with the royalties from true-crime books he had begun writing before he retired from NOPD. What he called a camp was actually built in a style I once referred to as Miami Drug Dealer-Modern. The two-story structure was stucco-over-cinder block, and the design involved nearly as much glass as concrete

Katrina forced water through this place as well, but it was the residence which could be rebuilt. The odor of spoiled food in the half million refrigerators pulled from flooded homes had also served to drive my mother from the city after the storm. She claimed that it smelled as though the city she could no longer recognize had died.

My mother used her own savings to pay for

repairs the insurance company wasted over a year trying to fight Tulip over in court, only to wind up settling for double the insured amount to keep Tulip from exposing their absurd damage appraisals and proving that they used engineering reports written and signed by non-engineers to exclude covered damages. Tulip had represented other homeowners and eventually threatened the worst offenders with the sort of class action lawsuits that would have bankrupted them. This fighting spirit was what had led to her reputation as a litigator only fools face in court.

My mother had supervised the renovations to the house while my sister made a project out of rebuilding me. The women in my life both oversaw the costly reconstruction of things they valued, but which would remain in harm's way. Any future hurricane storm surge is no less likely to wash through the house than I am to be killed while playing cops and robbers.

"Anybody home?" I shouted as soon as I stepped through the doorway to the main house. This being Saturday, I anticipated at least the maid being around. My mother only drove into the city for PEO meetings and lunch with a diminishing circle of sorority sisters. Tony was housed in the two-bedroom apartment over the empty boat house and doubled as my mother's personal chef. His absence was particularly curious since he lacked a driver's license.

"Miss Camille is on the patio," the maid called from where she was cleaning. My relationship with the service staff was considerably less formal than my mother insisted upon with any workers she paid. "Those people" needed to know their place.

My mother was indeed enjoying the March afternoon sun's unexpected warmth on the slate patio. She was reclined on one of the rattan seats facing the Rigolets waterway with a pitcher of gin and tonic and her cellphone within easy reach. She was dressed as though she were expecting company, however unlikely that was to happen, and had made sure her makeup was perfect. I could tell she'd recently had her graying roots addressed. She was typing on her iPad and paid me no mind until I blocked her sun.

"Consulting the Great and Powerful Oz again?" I asked to get her attention. My mother had begun consulting an online psychic, at unknown expense, rather than seeking psychiatric help in the wake of losing two houses and one estranged husband and me returning from the dead in quick succession. Her electro-swami's cryptic suggestions and observations were quite eerily similar to the fortune cookie wisdom my father voiced over the years, and that familiarity may have been what made her keep asking for this advice. Neither Tulip nor I were brave enough to suggest this possibility to her.

"As a matter of fact, I was." She switched the tablet off but held it on her lap. "He's begun giving me more advice for you and your sister than he does for me."

"What are today's words of wisdom?" I had to get past this to have any other conversation with her.

"That every beginning first requires an ending." She imparted these words and then took a sip of her cocktail while I worked on a flippant response. "He says you have to let go of your past in order to embrace what the future has in mind for you. New Orleans is a city full of fresh opportunities."

"And the Chinese symbol for opportunity is the same as the one for crisis." I said as a way to disengage from that topic. This is not correct, but it is repeated often enough to sound legit.

"Are you alone? How did you get here?" There was no motion for me to sit down so I just moved out of her sunlight.

"Bill gave me my own car."

"I guess that's a good sign." The uncertain tone in her voice was her way of fishing for details.

"We're going to try a Plan B. It means I get to work alone. He wants me to look for a guy who shot two men with a stolen pistol and then disappeared after his attorney got him released."

"Plan B sounds like a way to say your job will be to clean up other people's messes." It was as succinct of a summation of my situation as could be made. The harsh tone of her voice carried her personal opinion on this development, and she added a little snort to remind me that her unheeded suggestions to play nicer with NOPD might have avoided this.

"At least you'll see more of me. I'm moving out of the hotel in town and back to the boathouse." This was where she could have suggested that I use one of the three empty bedrooms in the main house, but she didn't.

"I hope it doesn't ruin your Wednesdays," she said and smiled. This was her way of letting me know she was aware that her brother, my Uncle Felix, had been arranging for me to meet one of the escorts he uses to blackmail politicians and lobbyists in a suite at the Monteleon Hotel every Wednesday. I had accepted the service when I first arrived home because I had not adjusted to my new face and felt no woman could stand to look at the scars from my

Special Forces career. The escort had rebuilt my confidence, but I stopped accepting her company after I entered the state police academy and recognized my own potential to be blackmailed by my uncle. "I'm sure your friend will appreciate having you as a roommate."

"Where is Tony, anyway? He wasn't at the boathouse when I dropped my bags off and he's not over here serving you tapas." I wanted her to know I could make sly cuts as well. She peered at me over the top of her reading glasses to let me know I was very wrong about that assumption.

"Tulip took him to the parade. They're probably drunk by now." Her sentiments about my sister escorting an Italian immigrant to the city's annual parade of inebriated Irishmen didn't need to be expressed aloud. "They'll likely be back late, if they aren't in jail."

The Hibernians' St. Patrick's parade traditionally ends with a raucous street party in the Irish Channel that stretches for blocks in any direction from a very small bar called Parasol's. I would have been in the midst of the throng as well were it not for my pending meeting with Avery.

"I have to meet the Chief in the Quarter later to discuss the case, so I'm going to take a nap and head that way. I just wanted you to know I'm staying here again."

"I'm sure you and your friend have lots to catch up on. You've all but abandoned him here. He needs to practice his English," my mother said with her tone of practiced drama.

It was undoubtedly best that I was closer at hand because Tony and I were trapped by the lies he had told Tulip about our personal connection while I lay sedated in the hospital in Naples, Italy. She believed he was a chef whom I had befriended while on leave and was unaware that he had driven me out of the ambush in time to save my life.

Tony had been an apprentice to a chef in Naples when members of Iraq's secret police forced him into a secret second career as an assassin of any exiled dissidents living in Europe who were calling for Saddam Hussein's overthrow. The Mukhabarat's recruiting pitch had been to threaten to kill Tony's Italian mother, and her entire family. Tony's Iraqi father had worked for them under the same threat before he was executed to keep his work a secret.

Tony had run a café in the Green Zone as a cover while he organized resistance to the Coalition troops occupying Baghdad during the Second Gulf War. I found him in a detention center and recruited him to help quell the insurrection he had helped to create. The first thing he did was to use the resources at our disposal to murder the men who had recruited him and to torture the man who executed his father for two days before slitting his throat in front of me.

I had been assured that our mission was backed by the State Department but discovered far too late that we were conducting an unsanctioned operation for a private contractor intent upon influencing the upcoming elections. Our unknown patron used the intel we gathered to control any politicians we linked to the attacks. The ambush I nearly died in was meant to silence our team, and I survived only because Tony fought his way out of the ambush to get me to a hospital and then smuggled both of us out of the country barely a step ahead of Iraq's new secret police.

3

I DRESSED IN A PINSTRIPED HUGO BOSS SUIT with a Jerry Garcia necktie and hung my freshly shined badge on my belt for the meeting with the Beauvoirs. I tested the Cadillac's handling on the two-lane road leading into the city and parked in front of the historic New Orleans Mint Museum on Esplanade Avenue. The Beauvoir's nightclub was in the middle of the last block of Decatur Street before it crossed Esplanade to become Frenchman Street. Frenchman Street is the locals' version of Bourbon Street, with small music clubs and plenty of places to eat and drink without being surrounded by the tourists the Beauvoir's place attracted. The couple's name was prominently stenciled above the waist-high curtains on the club's front windows in gilt letters. There was a uniformed detail cop beside the doorman who waved me through the open double doors, but his was on the valets and not on me.

"Ah, here is Detective Holland now," I heard Avery say to the couple he was making small talk with as I approached the bar. I imagine the couple had no idea what to expect when Avery had promised them the services of an investigator who would focus solely on their situation until it was resolved. I needed to appear to be considerably more empathetic than the NOPD detectives and ATF agents who responded to the shooting. They were probably more interested in the dead guys than any effect the shooting had on the couple or their business. I was, too, but my job was to act like I wasn't.

"I hope I haven't kept everyone waiting," I apologized unnecessarily. I was fifteen minutes early.

"I was just giving Janelle my Crawfish Monica recipe," Avery said. When you go to any party in New Orleans there comes a point when all of the men wind up in the kitchen exchanging recipes while the women argue in the living room about Saints player trades. "Cooter, I'd like to introduce Brett and Janelle Beauvoir."

I sized up the couple while they made their own first impressions of me. They were both in their early thirties. The husband was tall and slim with his straw-blonde hair gathered into a short ponytail. He wore designer rimmed glasses that gave him an unfortunately affected look, as though he was posing as himself in his own life story. The wife was a coppery redhead with a figure and smile that would turn heads, which probably explained the protective arm her husband kept around her, even in the company of armed men coming to their rescue. She was dressed rather provocatively, but she was about to go on stage to sing her set before her husband would emcee the burlesque show the couple used to pack the house.

We shook hands all around before Janelle motioned to the bartender and he stepped forward to mix me a Manhattan using an expensive selection from the bar's impressive bourbon offerings. I handed the husband my State Police business card, with my cellphone number written on the back. I had considered having it printed there, but writing the number by hand gave people the impression that they were getting my personal attention.

It had already occurred to me that our meeting here may have more to do with showing off a police presence than anything else. The couple were gracious hosts, but they were acting the part. Avery and I could both see that the pair were exhausted and anxious behind this façade of casually enjoying cocktails with us.

"So, tell me again, how are you connected to the local police department?" Janelle asked with an uneasy grin as she studied my business card. I took her questioning as a sign that Avery had failed to adequately explain the position that he had created for me hours earlier.

"I am brought in to handle special cases. FEMA is paying the State Police to place me at the Chief's disposal. He can assign me to focus on individual cases, such as yours. I will be working on nothing else than ending the situation you are in," I said brightly, with a minimal amount of smugness and sarcasm. It was something Avery appreciated my having worked on. My explanation seemed to reassure the wife more than the husband.

"I read your statements in the folder the Chief gave me, but I would like you to walk me through what happened one more time." I needed to see the couple's body language when they replayed the events. Body language is a far better storyteller than the spoken word.

The couple glanced at one another before the husband spoke up. "I was in the dressing room, but Janelle had just stepped through the curtains after her first set when a young man began shooting at a group of other men who were walking past the bar. The other men had guns in their hands, but they never fired a shot."

"So it clearly looked like self-defense?" I looked down the bar as if I were imagining the shooting. I knew the answer to my question, but I wanted to see how these two witnesses reacted to what might appear to be favoritism towards the suspect.

"That was how it was initially ruled," Avery reminded me before either of the Beauvoirs responded.

"How are you two still involved in any of this beyond witnessing the shooting?" I asked Janelle Beauvoir.

"The man has made threatening phone calls late at night, and he threw a brick through our front window a couple of weeks ago. He also tried to poison our dog," Janelle detailed the harassment. Her voice was breaking just thinking about their dilemma.

"He poisoned your dog?" The surprise in my voice masked my anger towards anyone who would use an animal to make an example or otherwise abuse one. Crime statistics indicate that crank calls and broken windows are par for this course but, the suspect was close to the point of being willing to murder one or the other of these two when things escalated to harming the family pet.

Brett covered Janelle's trembling hand on the bar with his own.

I sipped my cocktail to give the couple a moment to regain their composure. Avery would get a nice IOU for handling this, but what he wanted to do right then was to dump everything in my lap and get out of there.

"The report said that he calls every evening, but the physical attacks have only happened on Sundays?" I was at a loss to explain this odd combination.

"Yes, that's right. He was very polite when he first insisted that Janelle tell the police she wouldn't testify. He became very angry after she refused to do that. Then he pleaded a couple of time. He threatened to kill my wife during the last call," the husband explained. Janelle Beauvoir excused herself and went towards what I assumed was the green room near the rear of the high-ceilinged auditorium. Her husband waited until she was out of earshot to ask Avery a pointed question. "Is that what it took to get someone on this case?"

"Absolutely not." I defended my boss. "There is just not a lot of enthusiasm for a case that will probably never be prosecuted. He isn't likely to do any time for the shooting, and animal cruelty and intimidation don't justify investing NOPD's limited police resources. It is serious, and that is why I was assigned to the case."

I thought Avery was going to have a heart attack, but Beauvoir simply shrugged at the sad reality. I tried to soften the blow of what I had just said. "Like I said, this is the exact sort of case NOPD has me handle. How did he poison your dog? I didn't see it in the report."

"He put something on a piece of raw meat and threw it in the backyard last Sunday afternoon. I happened to be looking out the kitchen window when the bastard threw it over the fence. I went after the steak instead of the man. We're lucky that our vet lives around the corner and I was able to run Cory there in time for Doctor Amy to counter the poison."

"So your dog is still alive?" I asked with a level of empathy that surprised both the husband and Avery.

"Cory is still with the vet. She thinks he'll make a full recovery."

"Did the vet say what the poison was?"

"Nobody tested the steak. I threw it away and called the police. The uniformed officers did not take it with them when they came out to take the report. I can tell you that it smelled a little like he had poured kerosene or lighter fluid on it, which is probably why Cory just licked at it."

There was a lull in the conversation and Avery saw an opportunity to make his escape. "Detective Holland, I hope to hear from you soon."

Avery raised an eyebrow that only I could see from my position. It meant to call him with an update when I got home.

"Thank you so much," the husband said to Avery with genuine gratitude. He clearly understood he was out of his element dealing with the situation. Janelle was likely planning to hide until I was gone.

I was busy watching the detail cop and studying the interior of the nightclub when Brett spoke to me, and I gave him a blank stare. I covered by taking a sip of my cocktail while he repeated the question. "Okay, what happens now?"

"Well, I'd say you shouldn't answer your phone after dark if you don't recognize the number. Feel free to give him my number if he calls tomorrow," I told him bluntly, but as cheerfully as possible. "I'm also going to do an assessment of the club's security system. If someone was bold enough to plan to shoot somebody here once, they won't hesitate to do so again. Do you own a gun?"

"No, should I buy one?" Brett asked with the growing realization that he and his wife were dangerously unprepared for any further gunplay.

"Not if you don't already know how to use one," I shook my head. "Look, you are not in as much danger as you think. The guy I am after has a lot more to worry about than you do. All I have to worry about is finding one needle in one haystack."

"And you will do that before he comes back?"

"I'm very good at what I do," I gave him my most self-assured look. "You've already given me a couple of ideas of where to look. He should be easy enough to round up lurking around outside of your house next weekend if I don't find him this week. All the same, why don't you two stay in a hotel this weekend? Just to be on the safe side."

I shook the less than reassured husband's hand and headed for the door. I knew Avery would have preferred that I lie to the couple and tell them everything was going to be fine, but nothing was going to be alright until the guy I was looking for was back in custody.

4

I RE-READ THE POLICE REPORTS while sitting at the kitchen table in the boathouse on Sunday morning. I also studied the notes on the suspect for anything that might give me a place to start in my search. Tony had slept in. He went to bed still nursing the hangover and body aches he'd brought home in the pre-dawn hours. My sister drank him under a succession of tables, starting at Parasol's and ending at Snake and Jake's Christmas Club Lounge. I could only hope Tony did not form a lasting impression of the nature and quality of New Orleans' bars from an evening spent in dives, albeit iconic ones.

My quarry's name was Michael Alan Ferris. Michael was twenty-eight years old and a life-long resident of New Orleans. There was no record of any college or military service that would have taken him away from the city of his birth. He was a graduate of Gretna High School. This meant he was not someone with any experience or lessons in escape or evasion beyond eluding truancy officers. Michael Ferris's support network was limited to the immediate area, and the two people most likely to know anything were going to be his older brother and the girlfriend who had witnessed the shooting. The only other piece of useful information I was able to pull from the thin file was that Ferris used a pre-paid cellphone purchased from a convenience store in Houma to make the calls to the Beauvoirs. I have found much smarter, and far deadlier, people using less information.

The brother seemed the better choice of the two for questioning at this point. He was family, which means a lot to brothers raised on the Westbank. They grew up in a blue-collar community and surely earned their share of scars and stories hanging out on the proverbial street corners and sandlots with equally rough kids. It was the sort of neighborhood where a big brother was the best weapon to bring to a fight.

Barely three years separated the brothers' ages, but where Michael had little to show for his time since high school, his older brother had built something of an empire. Ralph Ferris owned a string of used car lots stretched between Gonzalez and Slidell, with the largest in New Orleans. I had seen his ads on TV. His niche was selling cars priced from five to ten thousand dollars by offering high-interest credit plans where you were expected to turn up every Friday with either cash or the car keys in hand. FEMA had, coincidentally, provided hundreds of thousands of people who had lost their vehicle to street flooding after the storm with checks for between five and ten thousand dollars to settle somewhere other than New Orleans.

New Orleans, and the entire storm-damaged region for that matter, was hoping people chose to relocate rather than come back to nothing. The areas where the poorest of New Orleans' citizens had lived weren't ready to handle the needs of so many people unaccustomed to fending for themselves.

New Orleans' City Council was doing everything it could to place hurdles in the way of anyone unable to support themselves after they returned. The city's flood damaged housing projects dating to the 1940s were slated for mass demolition and rental rates on the limited number of units available elsewhere in the city were climbing every week. What everyone in power seemed to miss was this was the only home tens of thousands of poor Black people, who spent the money intended to help them relocate on cars and steep rental deposits, ever knew.

Being underprivileged was always tough in New Orleans, but Hurricane Katrina had made it nearly impossible to survive. Neighborhoods lost their stores and schools, and public transportation was extremely limited. Charity Hospital was unlikely to ever reopen. The tourist and service industries most of them worked in were years from fully recovering.

The loss of trauma care was tragic as the number of gunshot wounds was on the rise as street gangs were beginning to do battle for turf the storm's evacuation had put up for grabs. There was plenty of legitimate minimum wage work available, but it was mostly hard manual work few of the young men who had moved back seemed particularly interested in doing. They found it easier and more lucrative to mug the Hispanics doing the work.

"Morning," Tony grumbled as he entered the living room from his bedroom at the front of the apartment. What I heard didn't sound at all like this word. Between his uncertain pronunciation and accent, it came out more like a grunt. I speak better grunt than Italian, but I had no objection to practicing one of the several foreign languages I could speak.

"Non per molto," I laughed and let him make his first espresso of the day in peace. He picked up the steaming porcelain cup and joined me at the table. "I think I might have a little something you might want to do."

Tony looked at me with as much gratitude and anticipation as he could muster with a hangover. I said nothing about the T-shirt he must have bought during his travels with Tulip. It was one of the large variety of shirts featuring derogatory re-imaginings of the acronym FEMA. This one read *Find Every Mexican Available.*

"I'd like you to do a security assessment of a nightclub in the Quarter. It's owned by the couple I am supposed to be protecting, and they are sitting ducks in there right now. They hired a detail cop Saturday night and all he did was watch the valets to be sure they didn't steal anything out of the cars. I walked right by him carrying a pistol. Anyone could have."

"Okay." It was one of the two words Tony had managed to learn in English that he could use to agree with someone without cursing. Way too many of his English language lessons were by way of American soldiers amusing themselves with hearing slang and profanity repeated back to them in what they considered to be a funny accent.

"You going to be alright? You look like a hot mess." His usually well-groomed thick, long dark hair had resisted his efforts to make a presentable appearance. His dark Sicilian eyes were bloodshot, and there were flecks of what I hoped wasn't vomit in the narrow strip of beard that circled his mouth and followed the sharp edge of his jawline. Mostly he looked vulnerable, and that wasn't something I was accustomed to seeing.

"I think I have figured out why you call something 'life' in English," he paused to take a sip of his espresso before finishing his thought.

"What's your conclusion?"

"Because you had already used the word 'crap' for something else." He was very proud of his joke, and I laughed as much from the unintentional wisdom in his opinion as I did from the delight that he took in having mastered enough English to make fun of the language.

"You're on to something. Go back to bed. I'll be back this afternoon, and we can talk about doing that walk-through sometime in the next day or two."

I gathered the stacks of sorted paper from the table between us and placed them neatly back into the file. I then placed the file in a black canvas messenger bag that I had begun carrying with me. It contained what I considered to be my essentials: my iPad, a digital camera and a digital recorder, a flashlight, batteries, and three extra clips of ten-millimeter ammunition for my Glock 20 pistol, a spring-loaded knife with a seven inch blade, a Leatherman multi-tool, and a medical trauma kit which included compression bandages treated with blood thickener, a sheet of plastic for sucking chest wounds, and two tourniquets. My sister refers to it as my 'bag of phobias' because it contains something to address just about everything that I feared might happen to me again.

5

MICHAEL FERRIS' OLDER BROTHER operated Ferris Wheels Automotive from a former warehouse on a side-street near Poydras to the lake side of the Superdome. The location was close enough to Mandina's Restaurant that I decided to have an early lunch of a shrimp po-boy and cold Abita Amber beer rather than confront the second-most likely person to know Michael's whereabouts on an empty stomach.

I ate standing at the bar and discussed the changes in the landmark cafe brought on by the storm with the bartender, starting with the place's very recent acceptance of credit and debit cards. It was becoming an accepted fact that locals were carrying debit cards rather than cash because the city was suffering from an increase in muggings. Businesses had to adjust to such post-Katrina realities or lose customers.

The remodeled décor was attributable to the damage done by four feet of standing water. This included newly installed central air, which improved the cooling but diminished the Old-South ambiance of the heavy Friedrich window air-conditioners that had been mounted over the doors and windows for as long as I could remember.

I steered the conversation to Ralph Ferris' dealership. The bartender suggested that I look elsewhere for a good car at a better price. The bartender had overheard multiple porters and line cooks complain that the dealership sold and re-sold the same cars. I recalled similar car lots near military bases where the used car dealer would take a down payment and finance the car at a rate and payment designed to be just barely too much for a soldier's pay, repossess the vehicle, and turn around and take the next enlisted man's down payment for the same car. I always wondered if any of the cars were ever paid for in full.

I found the Ferris Wheels dealership easily enough, thanks to a six-color graffiti-styled sign out front. I left my pullover and ballistic vest in the car and entered the building in a loose t-shirt, with my badge hanging from my belt beneath the fabric. I shifted my heavy Glock handgun from its waist holster to one in the small of my back that was also covered by the loose shirt. I did not want to approach Ralph as a detective, but rather as a random guy asking about his fugitive brother.

A young Black salesman, astutely sensing that I was more than likely there for reasons other than buying a car, politely steered me to the receptionist's desk situated just outside of the glass-walled sales office overlooking the show room floor. There was a CASH ONLY sign on the office window. Interesting.

The young Latina receptionist named Rosalita, whose fake smile was exceeded in size only by her breast implants, directed me to the building next door when I asked to speak to Mr. Ferris.

I accepted that any element of surprise I may

have hoped to exploit would be long gone by the time I finally located Ralph Ferris. The building she directed me to was the real center of the operation, where the magic of converting mere junk into saleable junk took place. A pair of semi-trailers full of used cars were being unloaded and the new inventory was being driven, and often pushed, up the ramp and into the shop.

I was not the least bit surprised to find the owner of the dealership was a beefy white guy dressed in khaki slacks and a starched dress shirt. He probably hired African American salespeople to give his customers the illusion of being ripped off by one of their own instead of just another greedy white guy with a Mercedes. I had to give Ralph some credit though; he was driving a top-of-the-line green Audi A8L sedan instead of a Mercedes.

"Nice ride," I complimented my quarry's older brother. Ralph grinned and stepped away from the porters who were detailing this sleek testament to German marketing. I remembered that the first generation of Audi cars were a nightmare for everyone but the car mechanics who put their kids through graduate school working on Audi electrical systems. "You probably bought it for the gas economy, right?"

Ralph wasn't quite sure whether he had just been insulted. I had the initiative in the conversation and continued to try to keep Ralph off balance by asking question after question about the Audi, as though I might be in the market for a new eighty-thousand-dollar car myself. Every question I asked that caused Ralph to stop and think made it harder and harder for him to remember any well-rehearsed lines about having no idea where his brother was hiding. I took him for the kind of brother that was going to throw in something about how distant the two of them were. This particular insult of a lie, which involves denying any familial bond, always bothers me more than most.

The one thing I had yet to find in New Orleans was any set of native-born siblings that genuinely didn't care what was going on in the lives of their brothers and sisters. I had almost perfected my bullshit meter for these lies. I based it on Newton's Third Law of Physics and assume that the effort they put into distancing themselves from the sibling I am looking for is proportionately inverse to how closely they are involved with that sibling's problem.

"So, Ralph," I finally said when I was ready to question him. "Do we talk here, or do you have a nice cozy office?"

"Talk about what?" Ralph sensed he needed to either stall or bluff me.

"Michael. What else is there to discuss?" I asked as though we had both known all along why I was there. "So, let me ask you again. Here or in private?"

Ralph led me through the garage to a door opening to the back offices of the dealership. The hallway we entered had a double key-locked heavy metal door to the right and a nicely paneled wooden one to the left that led into Ralph's office. Ralph either had unusually nice taste or a good decorator. I was just relieved that the office did not carry over the pimp-my-ride theme of the showroom next door.

Ralph's desk was mahogany, and very possibly an actual antique. The rug on the slate-tiled floor was a modern-day loomed variation of what was probably an authentic Persian design, but a better choice to have when a mechanic in greasy boots came by to talk. The art on the wainscoted walls were original oil paintings by a local artist named Michalopoulis, noted for his unique view of the Vieux Carre. They are like looking at New Orleans through the bottom of a soda bottle.

Ralph sat in the heavy leather chair behind the desk and motioned me towards one of the low-backed cloth seats in front of him. I moved away from the seat offered and sat on the Art Deco sofa beside the door. I leaned back and stretched my feet out in front of me, which did little to cover the distance to the massive desk.

"What do you want to know about my brother? I'm a car dealer, not his attorney," he snapped at me as though it answered everything. Ralph had probably practiced the line to sound like he was indifferent, but what he was actually saying was that he knew his brother needed an attorney. "Let me tell you what I have told everyone that has come looking for him. He and I have not talked that much since we buried our mom last year. I have this dealership, and a couple of other businesses, and Michael is making a name for himself customizing and restoring old motorcycles. I am not part of Michael's biker scene, and I really cannot think of anything to tell you that would help you find him. Personally, I think he got mixed up with some outlaw bikers dealing guns and took off. I don't know what else to tell you."

"Anything that you think might keep him alive would be a good place to start," I said after a moment's pause. He sounded genuinely clueless, but I suspected that he was trying to distance himself from Michael's situation. He could not do so.

"What the hell do you mean by that?" Ralph demanded to know.

I let the matter rest for just a moment. I noticed that Ralph's right hand had left the desk. His hand was likely gripping a pistol stashed in a drawer, or maybe the gun was mounted under the desk. I sighed as I stood up and approached the desk, from an angle rather than from directly in front of the desk, on the chance that the gun was mounted to shoot directly ahead. I did not respond to the question until I was sitting on the left corner of Ralph's desk and looking down at the Ruger pistol Ralph was fingering. We looked one another in the eye and then I finally broke the tense silence.

"I mean he is just waiting for a bullet at this point, isn't he? I show up and begin asking questions about your brother and you have yet to ask why I want answers. To me that means so many people have probably already come through here asking about him that you really don't care if it's a cop or somebody's goon anymore."

"Are you a cop?" Ralph belatedly asked, which only proved my point.

"What I apparently am, Ralph, is the only person looking for your brother that cares if he lives or dies," I deflected the question for the moment. "The cops don't care if he gets killed. The feds would only care because they could make a case against the gang that kills him. Everyone wants to make a bigger arrest with a bigger headline when they find your brother. The pals of the guys he shot want his hide, but what they really want is payback for what he did. Have you considered the next place they might look for satisfaction if they can't find him?"

I saw the lights flash on in Ralph's brain at that unconsidered possibility. He probably had absolutely nothing to do with his brother's actions. His problem was that there was no way out of this situation as long as he remained a link to Michael. My guess was that these visits and the possibility he was under surveillance were beginning to cause problems for his own shady business dealings.

"I know you have probably tried very hard to not know Michael's hiding place," I said just as calmly as I had spoken of the dangers Ralph may not have even thought about. "I also know that he has, or will, contact you for money and maybe even a car."

"Well I won't give him either one," Ralph declared in a cracking voice.

"Maybe not yet, but you will," I laughed and shrugged. "He's your brother, Ralph. You almost have to do something, don't you? Here is what else I know, just so we are on the same page. I know that the car you drive and the price tag on this office are beyond the means of the size of operation you are running. You also seem to be intentionally doing business on a cash-only basis. Cash businesses are tricky things, just ask any of the IRS auditors I could call. It makes me wonder if you are a smart enough guy to not let yourself get pulled down as an accessory or made into an accomplice to the first-degree murder charge hanging over your brother's head."

Ralph sank just that little bit lower in the chair he had hoped to use as a show of his authority and to take some measure of control back from the stranger in his office. He had no idea if the charges against his brother could be as bad as I was telling him, but I was right about one thing. Ralph wasn't about to take a percentage of any murder charges.

"I also know that if you don't take your hand off that damn pistol, I am going to slam the drawer on your wrist," I said in my first direct threat. I was relieved when Ralph closed the drawer. I was not at all surprised when the office door opened a moment later and a very large bodyguard stepped into the room. The guy was a bodybuilder, and I sized up my slim odds against him before I lifted the t-shirt to expose my detective shield and motioned for him to rest his hulking mass on the sofa. "Make yourself comfortable, we are almost done here."

The big man glanced at Michael and moved away from the doorway but didn't sit down. I pulled one of the business cards from my wallet and placed it on Ralph's desk. I placed an index finger on the card and slid it next to the MacBook laptop beside Ralph's right arm.

"I can protect your brother," I assured Ralph. "NOPD will throw him in Central Lock-Up and he'll get a shiv in his back the same day. The Feds would really like to pin his murder on the gang he crossed if they find him first."

"Anything else?" Ralph asked.

"Yeah," I said and paused at the door. "When is your brother's birthday?"

"I think it is June twelfth," Ralph said with some hesitation. "Why?"

"Because you just convinced me that you don't give a damn about your brother," I pointed out. "His birthday is July twelfth."

Ralph was silent as I spun around and walked out the door. The imposing thug was left wondering what he was supposed to do. Throwing me out was both unnecessary now that I was leaving on my own, and unwise as I turned out to be carrying a badge. Ralph probably hoped this was the last he would see of me, but he also knew he would continue to attract unwelcome visitors until one side or the other tracked down his brother.

I wandered through the dealership unescorted and paused for a second at the receptionist desk. I asked Rosalita for a piece of paper as though I was going to write a note but instead spent the next couple of minutes drawing the layout of the operation and studying the interaction between the salesmen and prospective customers. There were deals being finalized in a couple of the cubicles behind Rosalita, all involving customers that were dressed as well as they could be on what little money they made. Not one deal involved the punks in white T-shirts and baggy jeans that I pegged as likely gang members.

Six of them were loitering around a late-model Mustang convertible. I noted that all of the salesmen on the showroom floor were consciously avoiding making any eye contact with them, as though they knew these customers had come to see someone specific and not to shop for a car. One of the salesmen handed the Rosalita a stack of papers and a set of license plates that looked like they had had just been taken off of a trade-in vehicle.

"The buyers give you license plates. I always thought you were supposed to give them the plates," I said as though making a joke instead of an observation.

Rosalita laughed and smiled as she arranged what she had just been handed into a bright red folder. "Oh, no, it is something Ralph likes to do for his customers if they bring us a car as a trade-in."

"What exactly is it that he does for these folks?" I asked as though I were interested in her boss's acts of generosity.

"He has me turn their old plates in when I pick up the ones for their new car. Otherwise they could get in a lot of trouble for not turning them in."

"So, you'll turn those in later today?" I asked as though the answer was obvious.

"No, just once a week," she giggled and shook her head.

"Well, how nice of Mr. Ferris to think of that," I smiled warmly.

I was headed towards my car when Ralph and his bodyguard came onto the show room floor. They walked past Rosalita without saying a word and she most likely never mentioned the compliment I paid him. She probably just hoped Ralph would talk to the rough-looking guys standing by the Mustang so they would leave.

6

THE PERSON MOST LIKELY to know exactly where Michael Ferris ran off to was his girlfriend. I've always wondered what people are thinking when they leave someone that they have persuaded to love them to suffer the injuries from whatever comes tumbling downhill in their absence.

Ferris's girlfriend had done nothing wrong by attending a burlesque show with her boyfriend. She was likely as surprised as anyone when Michael shot two men to death right in front of her, but she had not abandoned him when the police arrived. She sat in the Second District police station for six hours waiting for the detectives to turn him loose, and she likely had not seen him since they got home, where he packed a suitcase because he knew it was just a matter of time before the serial numbers on the guns involved in his altercation led the police back to his door. Life on the run would have been no picnic for her, either, but it would have been far easier for me to track the two of them compared to finding one inexperienced but highly motivated fugitive.

Avery's file indicated that NOPD detectives were questioning her about Michael's whereabouts every couple of days. There had either been no request for a phone tap, or more likely the prosecutor's office was unable to convince a judge to help find their lost witness. Michael was unlikely to call his girlfriend's house phone anyway, but he probably did not have enough sense not to call her cellphone. Every call pinged his location. ATF agents had interviewed her once, as well, but only once. There was an outside possibility that they would keep a loose surveillance on her, if only because the ATF has a big enough budget that they can afford to over-estimate their quarry.

These were the thoughts that rattled about in my mind as I drove towards Annunciation Street in the Irish Channel. This neighborhood was barely a dozen blocks from the mansions of St. Charles Avenue, but light years away from them socially and economically. This was the area of four to six room shotgun-style houses that had been home to successive waves of new immigrants. Irish ditch diggers gave the neighborhood its longest lasting name but, after the storm, this neighborhood had become home to an uncomfortable mix of newly arrived young white professionals, the older blue-collar workers who had raised families here, retirees whose kids would likely sell their homes when they died, and families displaced from the flood-damaged public housing projects. The pre-storm residents were beginning to feel the pinch as those young white professionals who had moved from more expensive cities were nudging the rent and home prices out of everyone else's reach.

I approached Ferris's shotgun double, a one-story duplex split lengthwise, in an indirect manner. I hoped doing so would confound anyone following me. The streets between Magazine Street and the river are narrow enough that they run as alternating one-way streets to allow for parking on both sides of the street. I drove both of the streets running parallel to Annunciation trying to spot anyone watching the house through the block, as I would have done if I were I inclined to waste hours of my time. I assumed that if I could not see the house from either of these streets then nobody else was doing surveillance from there, either. The street to the river side of the address in question is a wide industrial truck-route called Tchoupitoulas. It did not present an opening to see between the houses, so I doubled back on the street above my target.

I could see the house in my rear-view mirror as I passed a playground on Laurel Street. A half dozen young Black adolescents were loitering by the entrance to the fenced off playground, but they looked like they were selling drugs and not waiting for a pickup basketball game. I also noticed a heavily modified Jeep Wrangler parked behind a gray Econoline van on the far side of the park.

Neon beer signs in the windows of a tavern across the street from the van opened the possibility that the owners of the Jeep and the van were just enjoying a cold beer in their favorite neighborhood bar, but the Texas plates on both vehicles pretty well ruled out that being the case. The bevy of stickers for the NRA and the letters GKGC-5 on the Jeep's personalized license plate lacked basic discretion.

Pals of the Texas gun club members that Michael crossed were the only people I worried about taking an active interest in Michael's girlfriend. I really hoped they were going to be patient, or would at least be gentle, in dealing with her. I didn't want this to end up as another case where some gang used the unprotected family or girlfriend of someone who crossed them to 'send a message' or 'leave their handiwork.' I just hoped that their very obvious presence was meant to do nothing more than instill enough fear in her to draw Ferris out of hiding.

I climbed out of the Cadillac and made sure the pullover covered the laser-sighted Glock on my hip. I locked the car and sauntered into the corner bar. It was unexpectedly cool and dark despite the large plate glass windows looking out on the street corner and the playground. The bar was empty but for me and the heavyset female bartender. She ignored me until I sat down and set money on the bar for the Abita draft that I gestured towards among the beer taps before I spun to look out the window.

"Nice Jeep out there," I said and pointed my beer towards the heavily modified vehicle.

"Lot nicer than the jerks driving it," she offered her opinion, as I hoped she might.

"They come in often?"

"Just to use the bathroom and payphone," she hissed. "They drag cases of beer from Rouse's into that van every day but don't spend a dime in here."

"Every day?" I faked disbelief. "Are they living in that van or what?"

"I dunno. They've been there a week now, but I can't say for sure why."

"I'll go find out," I told her and finished the beer in the chilled mug in three gulps. She was more than a little dumbstruck as I walked straight to the van.

I counted whoever was in the van to have at least minimal fear of the state police. I freed my Glock from beneath the pullover and made sure the badge on the lanyard around my neck faced the right direction before I simultaneously banged on the side and pulled open the right-hand rear door of the van, stepping into their possible line of fire with nothing but the flash of my badge and an untested faith in the state police's choice of Kevlar to protect me.

I had barely a second to survey the set up before the pair started to react, first to my presence and then to the badge. There was a small Canon high-definition video camera aimed at Ferris' house from the dashboard. Its output was being fed to the laptop computer perched on a table behind the driver's seat. I could not tell whether they were using the computer screen as a monitor or if they were streaming the video to interested viewers.

The van was packed with an upholstered sofa positioned behind the front seats and an inflatable mattress beside it, suggesting the pair were prepared to be there indefinitely. The interior reeked of sweat, spilled beer, and very faintly of antibiotic ointment. There was a trash bag full of food wrappers from the Wendy's a few blocks away and the empty beer cans from Rouses'. I interpreted this to be an indication that the van's occupants were from so far out of state that they were afraid to eat the local cuisine.

The pair looked to be no older than their early twenties. They both wore jeans and T-shirts promoting a gun shop in Port Arthur, but these were the only indications of them being the sort of firearm aficionados Avery had described to me. The one lying prone on the sofa had some sort of dark blue tattoo on the back of his left hand, but he hastily slipped this hand under the blanket covering his torso and legs.

Both men had sweaty, greasy, hair that was cut fairly short, but were unexpectedly clean shaven. The one lying prone on the mattress clutched what was probably a semi-automatic carbine under the covers.

His companion glanced to a pile of magazines beside the laptop computer that I assumed concealed his own weapon.

My element of surprise was gone, so I needed to avoid spooking the pair and causing them to shoot or run. Idiots like these two were easier to handle than the men who would surely replace them would be.

"Wow. Am I glad to see you two," I said and sat down on the ice chest full of beer beside the sofa. It was the first thing resembling a seat that I could find. "How's the surveillance going?"

"Excuse me?" the one at the desk asked as he hastily closed the laptop.

"You're the agents watching Michael Ferris's place, right?" I asked and pointed to the house I was headed to next. "I was told that ATF had two guys sitting on his girl, and here you are. Or are you DEA and watching the crack dealer on the other side of the park?"

I have always enjoyed forcing amateurs like this pair to simultaneously digest bad news, such as the presence of federal agents nearby and learning that they are sitting on some drug gang's turf. The spooked young men looked at one another in a hasty effort to decide whether to flee or fake their way through the next couple of minutes. They did not disappoint me with their choice.

"We're just watching the girlfriend. The locals have the dealer on one of their crime cameras," the one on the sofa bluffed me. I had no more reason to believe that NOPD's crime camera in the area was working than I did that these two actually were plainclothes Federal agents. "Nobody told us that you were coming by. I guess we need to work on our disguise, huh?"

"Start by buying your beer from the bar over there, and tip big. Be better neighbors," I advised them. Keeping the locals happy was a lesson I had learned the hard way halfway around the planet. I pointed at the double shotgun house down the street. "So, is the girlfriend home?"

"She should be leaving for work in about fifteen minutes," the one at the desk said and reopened the laptop. He had been careful not to interrupt the feed, which tipped me that the video signal was important to somebody watching it somewhere else. I couldn't imagine that the show being watched at the far end of their internet feed found it to be any more exciting than the live action version.

"Well, I need to have a word with her before she leaves. You guys keep up the good work. Give Hutchings my regards," I said as I stepped out of the van and started to shut the doors.

"Who?" one of the pair just had to ask.

"Gerald Hutchings," I patiently elaborated as though talking to people as stupid as I thought they were. "You know, the head of the ATF here in New Orleans, right?"

"Damn, I thought you said somebody else," the talkative idiot valiantly tried to cover. "Who should we say came calling?"

"Chief of Detectives, Bill Avery."

I kicked myself for pushing it with the pair. I had no more idea who the head of the local ATF office was than they did. I just wanted to see if they knew enough to either challenge the name I gave them, which was the name of my physical therapist, or were dumb enough to simply repeat it. I had avoided giving them anything useful about me to share with their leaders, but they would have me on the video feed in just a moment. I scrawled the license numbers of both vehicles on the back of one of my business cards as I rounded the van and walked towards the nearby residence. I would ask Avery to ID the owners the next time he debriefed me.

The rusty Chrysler convertible registered to Michael's girlfriend was parked across the street from her house. There was a restored antique Harley parked under the carport that led to Michael's customizing shop behind the duplex. The large cycle looked like something Michael might have been riding daily. I wasn't sure whether the girlfriend was making a passive-aggressive point in leaving it uncovered in his absence. I had a sudden hope of getting something useful from the interview if she was harboring some sort of anger or grudge that could be tapped into.

There was movement at the kitchen curtains when someone spotted me in the backyard. I turned and waved at the barely visible silhouette. A moment later an attractive brunette in an open necked tuxedo shirt and black tuxedo pants tucked into red ostrich skin cowboy boots opened the back door and came outside.

Whatever bad decisions and wrong choices Michael Ferris had made to this point in his life, convincing this woman to fall in love with him was probably the smartest thing he had ever done. The brief biography contained in the file I was carrying only put the facts of a life on paper. Julie Hart in person was strikingly beautiful without quite being gorgeous. Her skin was lightly freckled, her large eyes were as blue as an afternoon sky, her thick, shoulder-length dark brown hair was pulled back with a simple hair tie, and the man's tuxedo shirt couldn't hide her buxom figure. It also couldn't hide the heavy revolver in her waistband.

She was twenty-nine years old, had attended grade school and high school at Sacred Heart and had earned twenty credits towards a degree in architecture at Loyola before dropping out. She stopped attending classes the semester after Hurricane Katrina. Julie was now making a career as a waitress at one of the many Brennan-owned restaurants in the French Quarter. She and Michael Ferris had shared this house, which was rented in both of their names, for the past two years.

"Julie Hart?" People always smile when strangers call them by their first names, but almost nobody does when they are greeted by their full name. Julie, though, came up with a genuinely welcoming smile. It verged on a grin.

"Let me guess," she said with a faint singsong in her diction. "You're not here about a bike."

"No, but this is a great looking one," I admitted and ran a hand over the dusty cream-colored gas tank.

"It's a '47 Knucklehead," Julie informed me. "Do you know anything about motorcycles?"

"Not much, but I am something of an expert on knuckleheads. I'm Detective Holland from the state police," I said as disarmingly as possible. "I guess that I am one in a long line of recent visitors?"

"My favorites were the bounty hunters," she said and brought her left arm from behind her, holding a Mossberg pump-action shotgun in her hand. "They only came by the one time."

"And the two guys in the van up the street? Have they stopped by as yet?" I pointed, testing her awareness. I didn't think she was likely to shoot me, so I tried to ignore the cannon in her waistband as best I could. It's hard to do if you've ever been shot.

"They've been there since Michael took off," she shrugged. "The bartender you spoke to earlier is my aunt. She liked you."

"Good for you, Julie Hart," I grinned and handed her a business card. "Apparently it is too late to warn you that people may come looking for your boyfriend."

"Fiancé," she corrected me and looked at the card. She looked up and studied my face for a long moment.

"It occurs to me that you are probably pretty well set if they make a move. Can we talk inside?"

"Sure," she shrugged and led me back the way she had come. She stopped inside the doorway to pull her boots off. She also set the shotgun in the closet by the door. "We just had the floors done. Do you mind removing your shoes?"

The interior of the century old dwelling had been remodeled, opening what had been five rooms into three. The bathroom and bedroom were the only enclosed rooms, the kitchen, dining room, living room, and a former bedroom had been combined into one large space and the ceiling opened to show the original cypress cross members above the glossy heart pine floors. The windows had been replaced with double glazed fiberglass hurricane-proof windows identical in dimensions to the originals. The finish of the work and small touches of more obvious expense, like the marble kitchen counters, indicated that the money coming into this house likely exceeded what I approximated to be their combined legitimate incomes.

"This is a nice place," I complimented her as I

looked around the open area where she left me standing as she went into the bedroom with her boots in hand. I felt a little foolish holding my own shoes in one hand but saw no place to set them down. She had stashed the pistol in whatever hiding place she had for it in the kitchen. I assumed that there were additional firearms secreted about the house.

"Thank you. I did most of the work myself. Our landlord let us remodel in exchange for rent. I think he hopes we'll offer to buy the place. I love watching those shows on cable about doing rehabs and flipping houses. I just don't have the guts to do it professionally." Julie said through the partially open doorway to the bedroom. "I have to finish getting ready for work. Ask me whatever you want from out there, okay?"

"You really should consider being a decorator. You have a real talent," I shouted after her and realized that Julie had completely distracted me. I didn't expect to find Michael behind the sofa, and I also had no reason to believe she was going to blab anything to me that she had not already told everyone else. This did not make me feel any better about having my questioning completely derailed by her being so pleasant.

I studied the living room for clues. The large flat-screen television in front of the Stickley-style leather and wood sofa was tuned to a game show, but the volume was turned down. I turned and looked at the scant library, which was just a handful of literature selections left over from one or both of their years in high school, and a few big picture books on design and the history of motorcycles. The bookshelf had an empty spot. There was a gap in a line of photographs of the couple in happier times. The mail on the oak dining room table was addressed to both of them, largely bills and magazines. The Dell desktop computer and monitor were both turned off, as was the printer. I noted a webcam clipped to the top of the monitor.

The pictures on the walls were mostly enlargements of architectural and scenic shots one or the other of them had probably taken, but the mats and frames were professionally done. The rest of the décor included the locally requisite Jazz Fest poster – this one for the 2002 festival. I thought it might mark the year the couple had begun dating. The locks on the front door were secured. There were two Yale deadbolts in addition to the short chain. Neither of the locks looked newly installed, but this had not been a particularly safe part of town even before Hurricane Katrina changed the street's demographics.

"I suppose I should ask about the last time you spoke with Michael," I finally said loud enough to be heard through the slightly ajar bedroom door.

"I don't have his new number, or I would give it to you," she shouted back.

"New number?" I wondered if she had unexpectedly let something slip.

"He left his cell here when he left," Julie said. She emerged from the bedroom. Her feet were now in dressier work shoes instead of the boots that I had rather hoped she would wear. She turned and disappeared into the bathroom. She left the bedroom door open, and I noticed only one side of the antique brass bed seemed to have been slept in. There was no male clothing in sight. There was, though, an unusually large photo on the night stand of Julie and

Michael in wetsuits and diving under an oil rig on the nightstand. "I have not spoken to him on the phone since he left town."

"Perhaps by passenger pigeon, then?" I recalled the webcam on her computer. Michael could be hiding behind a VPN to video chat with her. She had only ruled out having spoken to him on the phone.

"They would just crap on everything," she said and laughed. Our shouting back and forth through half-open doorways had the effect of negating any sense of pitch or inflection in her responses. I sensed that she knew this and had arranged the conversation accordingly. "Michael just wants his life back, and I want my fiancé back."

"Well hiding isn't likely to get that done," I said.

"Turning himself in isn't likely to, either. Is it?"

"It would be a wise first step. Nobody can protect either of you indefinitely in your current situations, and you probably don't want to live the rest of your own life alone and having to worry about who shows up looking for him."

"So, what then? I'm supposed to tell him what a great guy you are and to surrender and you'll fix everything?" she shouted, but I heard the scorn in her voice.

"Well, I do fix things," I suggested. "It just depends on how badly broken they are and how much someone wants them fixed. My task is to find Michael and bring him in, and that will be voluntarily or involuntarily."

"You mean dead or alive?" she shouted again, now a little angrier. I pressed my hands to either side of the bathroom door frame, feeling tired of her maneuvering this conversation.

"If I wanted him dead, I'd just go drink beer with

your aunt all afternoon until the Texans in the van find him or he gets shot in a traffic stop. From what I know of the case, he could get a pretty easy deal on the shooting if he gives up the guys who he bought the gun from. There are worse things than witness protection, believe me," I made my case to the one person I thought might deliver it.

There was a brief pause and then Julie opened the door. Her makeup was minimal, meant to accent her eyes and to conceal the freckling across her nose. She was startled by my looming presence. I realized I had unintentionally scared her enough to see behind the bold mask she wore so well. I backed up a step and brought my hands up in a show of peace.

"Can you give me your version of what happened at the Beauvoirs' club?"

"Three guys came through the door and headed straight for Michael. He shot two of them and the other guy dropped his gun and hobbled out."

"How did your boyfriend know they were coming after him? It sounds like it all happened pretty fast." I was impressed with his fast reaction to the situation. It didn't sound like he had hesitated for a moment before defending himself and Julie.

"Beats me. He saw the guns and pushed me to the floor just before he started shooting."

"Maybe they weren't after him," I was talking to myself now. Everyone assumed they were after him because they were the only ones he killed, and because his gun matched those of the dead guys. Julie just shrugged at this idea. "What were you two doing there, anyway?"

"I was thinking about trying out for their revue. I heard it pays better than waiting tables." I caught myself before I offered an opinion on what I saw as her promising future in burlesque. "They only started doing shows in the last couple of months. I hear their nightclub is losing a lot of money. They don't book enough local bands and most of the local musicians don't think she's a good singer anyway."

This was an interesting rumor not to discuss with the Beauvoirs the next time I saw them. It did not strike me that their financial situation had any connection to what happened that night. Still, the possibility that one or the other, or both of them, had been the intended targets didn't seem nearly as far-fetched as I would have liked it to be.

Julie didn't seem to have given the incident any further thought than being glad that it wasn't her or Michael lying in the morgue. I was confident that Michael had told her what he knew before he skipped town or had at least told her enough that she made sure to always be situationally aware while stuck here by herself.

"Look, you have my card. My cellphone number is on there. However you are in touch with Michael, let him know that I am looking for him, and that I can help him get ahead of this instead of his having to be the fox in everyone else's fox hunt," I said evenly. She remained where she was. "I'll even give you a sign of good faith and get rid of the guys in the van for you."

"How are you going to do that? They aren't breaking any laws that you can hold them for, are they?" She sounded unconvinced.

"I didn't say that I was going to arrest them," I pointed out. "I just said I would get rid of them."

"What are you going to do, shoot them to get me to trust you?"

"Would that work?" I laughingly inquired. Julie

clearly could not tell if I was joking. I was starting to worry her.

"It would scare the piss outta me," she admitted and slipped past me to go to the bedroom. I waited for her to slam the door, but she had only gone to get her tuxedo jacket and purse. "I need to get to work."

"Okay, I'll walk you out," I stated rather than offered. It wouldn't hurt for the guys in the van to see her talking with a cop, even one as strange as I was proving to be.

Julie locked the front door before I walked her to her car. Both of us glanced towards the van as we crossed the street. I held her car door for her and closed it once she was buckled in. She waved my card at me and tucked it inside her jacket pocket and smiled, but not as comfortably as she had when we first met. I stood in the street to block the van as Julie pulled out and drove away. The van remained parked, perhaps because of my presence but more likely because they knew Julie's routine so well that they knew where she was headed. I made a mental note to drive by her place of work later and see if there was a van parked there, as well.

I walked back to the bar and came out a moment later with a six pack of Heineken in a paper sack. I left my Glock, badge and pullover in the car before I walked towards the four junior entrepreneurs still on the corner. They ignored me at first, probably thinking I was just another drunk white guy headed home with my liquid supper. One of them may have had a quick thought that they did not remember ever having seen me before, but all of them apparently decided I was neither a potential customer nor any sort of threat as I approached them. It was the way that I stopped so suddenly in front of them that caused just enough confusion that their reaction was to assume they were being attacked and reached for their concealed weapons. They were all armed.

"Hey, chill," I grinned and spoke in an almost conspiratorial voice. I did not reach for my pistol as they each gave away where they carried a pistol. "I just need a minute of your time."

The youngest of the bunch, a pudgy Black kid about sixteen years old, snatched the bag that I offered them and was surprised that it held cold beers. He twisted lids off the bottles and handed them to his cohorts, but he did not offer me one.

"What kinda cop are you, anyway? You gonna take our money or something?" the tall one I had already pegged as the leader finally spoke up. It was telling that they suspected a middle-aged white guy wanting to talk to them of being a crooked cop. This validated my argument with Avery that NOPD had lost the trust of the city's minority communities in the wake of Katrina when they chose to treat everyone as potential looters rather than as fellow citizens needing food and water.

"Do I really look like a cop?" I sneered and lifted my shirt. I had their attention but also saw that most of them were still ready to draw on me at the slightest provocation. Every crazy drunk around here knew better than to stop and talk to thugs like them. "I don't care what you're doing out here. I just need a favor."

"What's the favor?" one of the other boys asked.

"I own the bike shop over there," I lied and pointed vaguely towards Uptown. I really hoped that none of them knew Michael or that there was even a bike shop in the next block. They said nothing and I pressed on. "I have to leave town for a couple of weeks, and I need someone to keep an eye on my place and my girl. We just found out she's pregnant and she's really worried about being alone right now."

"Yeah, bitches be like that," one of the others unexpectedly commiserated with me. "Remember when Juanita got herself pregnant and it was all I could do to get outta my place at night?"

"I know, man," I said and shook my head, trying to draw them further into this improvised story. "I just need someone to keep an eye on the place. You know, someone to walk by a couple of times a day. Let people see you so they know someone's guarding her. It's worth a hundred bucks a week."

"Yeah, we'll do that for you," the leader decided. He was probably nineteen years old, basketball-player-lanky and strong. He looked to the vinyl-sided house I was pointing towards and nodded that he understood the address. "But it'll cost two bills a week."

"Fine, as long as nothing happens while I'm gone." I acted as though we were actually in negotiations. "I'll be back in two weeks and pay you then."

"Huh uh, you pay right now." The dealer stuck his hand out, palm up.

"Right," I cautiously balked. I didn't want to lose their help, but I also wasn't going to actually give money to a street gang. "Are you going to give me my money back if I pay you and something happens? If nothing happens while I am gone, I'll put five hundred bucks in your hand when I get back, how's that for a deal? You won't have any trouble collecting because you know where I live."

"What do you think's gonna happen?" the kid

asked. The price for protection had escalated quickly but I was the one who had last raised the price.

"I don't know, but that van never used to park there. I don't think it's the cops. For all I know, some gang plans to move on your corner. My girlfriend is sure they are casing our place and plan to rob us while I'm gone. I just don't want anything to happen to my girl, okay?"

"That van?" the leader ignored me and turned to look at the unmarked panel van. I pointed at it and confirmed that it was what worried my imaginary girlfriend.

"That's the one. Just keep an eye on it and I'll see you in two weeks, okay?" I asked and started walking away. The dealer nodded but kept his attention on the van, now squinting at it as though he had some sort of x-ray vision.

I walked back to my locked car and drove away. I figured one of a number of scenarios would play out fairly soon. There was the possibility that the sudden interest in the house by another bunch of punks would shake Julie's hard shell enough to call me in a much more cooperative mood. There was now the certainty of some sort of confrontation between the dealer and the duo in the van, and that could work any of a number of ways. The Texans could tell the dealer the truth and he might believe it, but more likely there would be no discussion at all before the bullets started flying.

I wanted to disrupt the routine that Julie and her stalkers were settled into, because it was a static situation that was not likely to change on its own, and I hate static situations. Dynamic ones are always so much more interesting and provide opportunities to exploit.

7

THE PHOTOGRAPH I spotted on Julie Hart's bedside table was my best lead on where Michael Ferris was holed up. Ralph wasn't going to be of any help to me, and I didn't have enough time to figure out how he might be helping Michael, or even if he was. The photograph was a thin lead, but it was enough to pursue in the absence of anything else.

I started in Metairie, where there was the largest concentration of dive shops. A couple of them had been damaged or flooded by the storm and never reopened, and I struck out at all of the others. My father paid for my SCUBA certification at Harry's Dive Shop for my fifteenth birthday, so I lost an hour catching up when I recognized one of my instructors. He was long retired from teaching but liked to hang around the store and talk to new divers.

After wasting most of the morning, I realized I should have started on the Westbank. The Ferris brothers grew up in Gretna and were most likely to do business where they were familiar with the people running a place. Temento's Dive Shop in Westwego has been in business since the late 1950s and still supplies most of the area's commercial divers with their equipment.

The middle-aged salesman who approached me as I browsed the display of buoyancy vests was disappointed when it turned out I was looking for someone and not something. He was hesitant about touching the photograph I handed him of Michael Ferris, even after I'd shown him the State Police badge on my belt. He finally gave it a good long look before he tried to convince me that he had never seen Michael. He held onto the photograph as he led me to the clerk working behind the counter and handed him the picture.

"That's Mikey Ferris. What the hell has he done now?" the clerk immediately laughed. He could tell that whatever Michael was involved in wasn't being laughed off if a state police detective was asking around about him, which made Michael's situation even funnier to him.

"He messed up," I simplified my explanation. It was a close approximation and was an answer they would understand.

"Have you talked to his brother?"

"Ralph put as much distance between he and his brother as he could." I sensed this clerk had a personal background with one or both brothers that went beyond the store. He looked to be about the right age to have gone to school with one or the other of them, and the Westbank they grew up in was a small enough place that he may have even been a neighbor.

"Sounds like Ralphie," the clerk didn't laugh this time. "Why are you looking for Mikey here, though?"

"I'm playing a hunch. I think he may be looking for work as a diver. He's on the run but he still needs to make a living."

"You might have better luck asking around some

motorcycle shops," the clerk offered. "He is pretty well known for his custom work."

"That's why I think he'd assume it would be the first place someone would look for him. I'm going with the idea that he must have some other useable skill." The clerk and I stared at one another for a moment. I was now sure that Michael's situation was a local topic of conversation and that this guy knew at least as much about Michael as was in my files.

"Well, he isn't working as a commercial diver. He's only got a Master Diver's certification, and that isn't anywhere close to what even the shallow water outfits require," the clerk finally advised me. It sounded a lot like he was trying to wave me off this line of thought, but I was willing to trust his opinion if not his intentions.

"I don't know, Pete, he could be working with some of those guys still pulling boats out of Barataria Bay." The older guy who spoke up behind me was wearing a polo shirt with a charter fishing boat's name embroidered above one breast and Captain Dan over the other one. He was gray-haired and well-tanned and looked exactly like what I thought a charter boat captain should look like. He was waiting to buy several jugs of something called Corexit.

"Pulling boats?" I had no idea what he meant by this term, but everyone else seemed to be nodding in agreement that it was a viable possibility.

"FEMA's been paying local salvage outfits for any boats they pull out of the channels or drag back into the water from wherever they wound up on shore. Most of the shrimp boats and charter boats along the coast wound up one place or the other after the storm," the captain explained. I now recalled the photograph of two massive shrimp boats blocking

Route 23 in Empire the day after the storm.

"So they'd hire someone like Mikey?" I used Ferris' local name to maintain the illusion that this was a conversation about our mutual friend and not a detective looking for a fugitive.

"It's not that tough of work and there's not near enough divers around," the clerk added his two cents. "But the sort of outfits he would be working for are going to be hard to track down. They're not in the phone book or got a website."

"I guess it's still worth a shot," I shrugged. I didn't want to seem doggedly determined lest one of these guys worry enough to tip off Michael. I needed him to feel safe wherever he was, so he didn't change his new routine. It was hard enough developing a lead even this thin. Having to start all over again with less to work with would make it impossible to find him in the time frame I had been given. I caught a whiff of something that smelled a lot like kerosene and traced the odor to the gallon jugs Captain Dan set on the counter. "What's that stuff?"

"Corexit. It's a petroleum dispersant. You'll probably be able to track your guy down by the odor of this stuff on his gear. The fly-by-night outfits get around the Coast Guard regulations about having to contain any oil and fuel from any submerged boats by soaking the spills with this stuff. It breaks up oil slicks by making the oil settle to the bottom." The stranger was being so helpful that I didn't ask what his own use of the product was going to be.

The piece of meat Brett Beauvoir claimed smelled like kerosene might well have tested positive for this chemical, and knowing its purpose nudged me just that little bit forward in my search for Michael Ferris.

I thanked everyone for their time and headed out the door but glanced back through the store's plate glass front windows to see their reaction to my visit. The topic of discussion appeared to already be on something else by the time I made it to my car.

8

I NEEDED TO MEET CHIEF AVERY to do our first debriefing on my progress. He wanted to meet at the walk-up barbecue shack across the street from the criminal court building and police headquarters on Tulane Avenue. I arrived ahead of Avery and parked on the street directly in front of the barbecue place rather than in one of the pay-lots behind the bright yellow shack. I was sitting at a painted wooden picnic table near the huge drum smokers when I noticed a black Mercedes s550 slowing as it passed the sedan Avery had given me barely three days earlier. The driver parked and approached the BBQ joint.

He was dressed in a well-tailored pinstripe suit and expensive loafers. While it is not at all out of the question that anyone dressed this nice would choose BBQ as their mid-day meal, the way this character kept his eyes on me made me keep my eyes on him. He seemed hungry for something besides pork ribs.

"Are you Detective Holland?" he asked once he stood across the table from me.

"I am" I said but offered nothing else. I did not want to start a conversation with the stranger.

"I would like to speak with you about Michael Ferris. I feel he may be in danger," the man said and handed me his business card.

His accent sounded local, but he was more likely from Brooklyn because he would have had an easier time finding a bespoke tailor-made suit there than here. Attorney Daniel Logan looked about forty-five and he stood under six feet tall. His name was English, but his face looked Slavic, though any sharp angles were obscured by pounds of fat. His dark, thinning hair was slicked back, and he seemed to be hoping that using his charm and a friendly expression might persuade me to cooperate with him.

"We share the same concern. I cannot discuss the case with you because you are not his attorney," I said.

"What makes you say that?" he demanded.

"Michael cannot afford an attorney who drives a six-figure Mercedes and Ralph wouldn't pay for an expensive attorney to defend the kid brother whose birthday he cannot remember. My guess is you work for the guys that Michael shot, and I suspect that you tracked me down in hopes I would say something to help you find him before I do."

"You get all of that from my car?" Logan asked. I had clearly knocked him off balance.

"Yeah," I said flatly. "I have moved on to why a guy with a likely Russian heritage is named Logan."

"I was adopted," Logan explained. He was clearly uncomfortable with this being the new topic.

"Been here long?" Avery interrupted our conversation. I had watched Avery position himself behind Logan's left shoulder.

"No. I've just been explaining why I won't share what I know with Mister Logan here, I said.

"I was just leaving. Perhaps we will speak again,"

mumbled and retreated.

"You want to avoid that guy," Avery needlessly warned me. "You can ask your pal Katie about him."

"Katie was Tulip's babysitter, not my friend. We haven't spoken since I got back in town," I told him.

"Why not?" he pressed. I did not like this topic any more than Logan liked talking about his past.

"She is married now," I offered as a lame excuse. He shook his head. "And I cannot tell her where I was or what I did for the last decade, or where I got this face. I started a clean slate when I got home."

"Fine, he huffed. "How's the search going?"

"I think I know where to look for Michael. I may have also stumbled upon something else. I think his brother is running a getaway car rental service."

"Focus on the matter at hand," Avery instructed me. "You are too new at this to be pursuing crazy ideas like that."

"Jumping down rabbit holes is what military intelligence is good at," I said to remind him of my background. "Ralph's dealership turns in the plates on any local trade-ins once a week. This gives them a few days' float to use them as they see fit. I suggest looking at any cases where a witness gave a license number that did not match the car they saw."

"Fine. I'll have somebody look into it," the Chief shrugged. "What do you have on Michael?"

"There are two guys watching Michael's house from a van parked down the street, but they haven't made a move against his fiancé yet. I don't know if they are waiting for a special moment or orders, but I am working on getting them moved off the house," I summarized the handwritten talking points on the notepad I had pulled from my messenger bag. "I think they are most likely connected to the gun club the ATF thinks stole the guns that started this whole thing. One of them has what looks like prison ink."

"Explain what you mean by 'moved off the house.' How do you propose to do that?" I had hoped that part of my report would slip past him.

"I suggested to the drug dealers down the street that the guys in the van might be getting ready to make a move on their corner."

"What did you expect to accomplish by doing that?" Avery vented more than a little exasperation.

"With any luck the drug dealers will shoot up the van. The guys in the van may kill the drug dealers instead, but that's a risk we can accept. The van will be pulled off the house either way, and there won't be any sort of indication that the police played a part in doing so if the guys from Texas look into it."

"You don't think they will just replace the van? Ferris did kill two of their men, after all." He knew it was too late to stop what was already set in motion.

"I think whoever gave Michael the pistol he used in the shooting thinks he might roll on them, which suggests to me that my time would be better spent on finding whoever *that* person was."

"What about the girlfriend?" Avery asked and ignored my second suggestion that we change the focus of my investigation.

"Julie seems fearless. She knows she is being watched, but she has good door locks and Michael left her with quite an arsenal. She keeps the house suspiciously immaculate. Hers is the only toothbrush in the bathroom, and only one side of their bed looks like it's been slept in. The picture she keeps closest to her is one of she and Michael scuba-diving near the oil rigs, probably off Grand Isle."

"What's any of that mean?"

"Well, let's see," I assumed my familiar briefing role and flipped the pad to a clean sheet of paper. I made a circle of boxes, one for each point, and then drew lines between them to make a central point of intersection. "Michael only shows up on Sundays, but he calls to threaten the Beauvoirs almost every night. The chemical he used to poison the Beauvoirs' dog supposedly smelled like kerosene. So does at least one of the dispersants they use on oil and gas leaking from sunken boats. Michael has never lived outside of New Orleans, so I doubt that I will find he has any sort of support network outside of the area."

Avery sighed. "I am hearing a lot of theories, but I am not hearing anything that sounds actionable."

"I am going to look for him closer to the coast," I declared and tapped my pencil on the intersecting dot on my notepad. "He bought his burner phone in Houma. I think he went there to find work doing salvage diving."

"And if he isn't there?" Avery asked, clearly questioning my judgement. He resisted the urge to laugh at my confounded reaction to his doubts.

"I'll tell you what. You can pick up the tab at K-Paul's if I hand Michael over before French Quarter Fest." I had already discovered that betting food was the best way to make NOPD's omnivorous Chief of Detectives to take me seriously.

"You figured all this out in two days' time," Avery laughed as he picked up the pad and looked at my crude diagram. "Nobody else came up with your salvage diver idea."

"Nobody has had as much interest in finding him," I pointed out as I stuffed the notebook back into the messenger bag. "I am serious, though, about Ralph Ferris. He is into something illegal."

Avery grunted and rose to leave.

"Wait. I need to ask you for a couple of things. Get a search warrant for Michael's place and have your guys see if his dive gear is there without making it look like that is what they are looking for. They should probably run the serial numbers on any guns they find as well. Also, can you run some license plate numbers for me, and can you get me Michael and Ralph's cellphone records for the last two months?"

"That takes you further back than the shooting." I'd handed him a laundry list of things to get but he was sharp enough to catch the smallest details.

"I want to see who he was talking to before this started. I don't believe Ralph's story about he and his brother seldom speaking to one another. I also want to see whether either of them has ever spoken to the bozos in Texas." I found the card with the plate numbers written on it and shoved it towards Avery.

"I'll take care of this first thing when I get back in the office. The search warrant and cellphone records may take a few days," Avery informed me. "In the meantime, do what I tell you and keep away from Daniel Logan. He showed up after the storm and began getting cases from before Katrina tossed because the evidence was lost in the flood. He has put some very dangerous criminals back on the streets. An unusually high number of witnesses in any of his cases that went to trial either recanted their testimony or disappeared entirely."

"Not a problem," I assured him. Daniel Logan was less interesting to me than was his interest in a case in which he did not represent the defendant and refused to identify his real client.

We turned our attention to the menu board.

9

TONY AND I MET THE BEUAVOIRS at their nightclub Wednesday morning to do the promised security walk-through. It was a way to reassure the couple that I was actively working on the case and that I genuinely cared about their safety. Both things were true, but not nearly in equal amounts. I felt no physical threat would likely be made against either of them during the week based on what they told me of the harassment pattern, but that there was a very strong likelihood of something happening on Sunday. I planned my week around trying to find Michael Ferris between Monday and Friday, having Avery increase patrols around their house and nightclub on Saturday while I took the day off, and then personally watching their house all day Sunday.

Tony touring the nightclub was a dog and pony show as far as I as concerned, but tony played his part well. Today he was wearing an Armani suit and had one of my pistols, unloaded, in a leather shoulder holster bulging menacingly from just under his left armpit. He looked considerably more formidable than he did when he was hung over at our breakfast table on Sunday.

"This is Anthony Vento. He is an international

security consultant I have worked with, and he has agreed to look over your operation and make suggestions where he sees any issues," I told the Beauvoirs when we met them outside their nightclub. Tony gave them each a firm handshake before Brett turned to unlock and open the door. Luckily, they didn't ask any further questions about his background in security work. Brett and Janelle led the way inside. Brett pulled me aside as Janelle began giving Tony a tour of the main bar area and showed him where the shooting occurred.

"How much is your guy going to charge us?"

"His advice is free and doing what he tells you will be an investment." I tried to make the second part of this sound like more of a joke than it was. The things I would have recommended, just from what I could see off-hand, would cost thousands of dollars. I noted that his first concern was money, confirming what Julie Hart had told me about their finances.

Everything that was wrong with their security was immediately evident, but none of it was likely to be changed once the couple balanced the cost-to-benefit ratio. The two front windows were tempered but easily broken. I was guessing that neither of the panes were rated as hurricane glass. The double doors had insufficient bolts to hold them in place against anyone ramming them. The bartender had a panic button, but it was located at the door end of the bar. He would have to run towards anyone with bad intentions to press the alarm. We had taken three steps inside and I had already found this many serious issues.

Brett opened the double swinging doors beside the service-well end of the bar and showed us the beer cooler and store room for the liquor.

"What's upstairs?" I asked when I spotted the antiquated freight elevator near some dry storage racks. It was so old that it had a wooden lift-gate that had to be lowered for the elevator to operate. The elevator had once carried furniture from the top floor to the showrooms on the lower levels, but that was in a different incarnation of the building.

"I have no idea," Brett admitted. "Our lease is only for the ground floor. We had hoped to open a private club on the second floor at some point."

I chose not to share my opinion on the viability of that ambition. One part of Tony's purpose in being here was to try to verify what Julie told me as best he could. I had no reason to inquire about such things within the scope of the narrow mission I was supposed to be handling, but I was beginning to think there were more parts to this manhunt than I believed even Chief Avery grasped.

I watched Tony count the security cameras. It would take him a little longer than it took me to realize there were no hidden ones. The cameras were positioned to be as obvious as possible, as though deterrence was their true purpose. Their field of view was narrow and few of them gave overlapping angles, which meant there were going to be coverage gaps between the cameras.

"Are your cameras motion-activated?" Tony asked. His English had less of his Italian accent today. I knew it was a struggle for him, which was why we rehearsed the questions he would ask. I was the one who wanted the answers, but I didn't want to be the one who poked his nose into their operation. They were not suspects, and the more I personally made them feel like fools about their security, the more they might feel I believed they deserved what was happening to them. Tony was here to do all of that, but more tactfully than I would have.

"No, the landlord insists that we turn them on when we get here and then turn them off when we leave," Janelle said. She sounded like she knew how suspicious this sounded, and she wanted us to know that limiting their use wasn't their idea.

"So, you have no idea what goes on when you are not here?" Tony asked them to verify. He shot me a look to be sure I was following the conversation. Anyone could pick their locks, or use a key from the landlord, and have full run of the entire building in their absence. The building's owner could be using the top two stories for any number of purposes they would never know about. "How long do you store your records?"

"What records?" Tony's question was lost on Brett for a moment, until he sorted out a good translation. "Oh, you mean the recordings. The cameras run on a loop. They begin recording over the old stuff every twenty-four hours."

This time the couple saw the look Tony flashed me. They clearly felt they were being judged, but their security measures were no worse than the average small business that did the bare minimum expected of them by their insurance company. They didn't understand that it is the businesses that think this narrowly which become the ones that criminals target.

It was anybody's guess how many people might have been hurt in the nightclub had the three men Michael shot been the first to open fire. The nightclub's poor design did not allow for a way to block access to the dressing rooms from the stage wings. Worse yet, there was a door to the dressing room corridor which could be accessed from the vestibule containing the restrooms. A privacy sign on the door was their primary means to secure it. The door itself could be locked from the dressing room side, but it had a button-lock on the door knob and not a deadbolt. The delivery door opened onto Decatur Street and was similarly poorly secured. There was a heavy latch bolt on it, but the last person to use the door, likely a beer deliveryman earlier in the week, hadn't bothered to have anyone lock it behind them.

"I've seen enough," I said to excuse myself once we retraced our steps from the windowless dressing rooms to the stage. "I'm going to leave you in Tony's capable hands. He can make some suggestions to improve your security. You will then have to decide for yourself whether to take his advice."

10

I TOPPED OFF the Cadillac's fuel tank and headed west on Interstate 10 with Wednesday's lunch-time traffic. I ordered a hamburger at the McDonald's in Houma and read the employment ads in the Houma Courier while I ate. There were a handful of ads from companies looking for hourly laborers, but none for divers. There were also no companies advertising their services to raise any sunken shrimp or charter boats. My theory had hit a snag.

The region south of I-10 has always been a good place to hide. The oil fields and fishing industry have long been havens for anyone on the lam. This was the home of pirates, privateers, and anyone else trying to disappear among like-minded loners.

The pirates and privateers had made a good living robbing the heavily laden vessels heading to and from New Orleans, but it was Jean Laffite's gunpowder and cannon that had saved New Orleans in the War of 1812. His reward for this patriotism was a pardon and expulsion from Louisiana. It was encounters with outside authorities such as this that still encourages the locals to ignore what their neighbors are up to and to shield one another against any inquisitive strangers with badges.

It took only a few minutes to locate the Conoco convenience store near the Southland Mall where Michael Ferris had purchased the cellphone that he was using to pester the Beauvoirs. I showed the clerks Ferris's driver's license photograph and received shrugged shoulders and insincere apologies when nobody admitted they had sold him the phone.

A check of the store records indicated that one of the clerks who was present had made the sale, but he remained adamant about not recognizing the man in the picture. The manager apologized that the VHS videotape with the security camera footage from that date had already been recorded over at least twice.

I stepped outside and considered the possibility that this photograph no longer applied to Michael Ferris. Ferris had likely adopted some sort of disguise by the time he arrived in Houma. Nobody's driver's license photo is ever their most complimentary likeness, and Michael may have done nothing more to disguise himself than to pull a ball cap down to his ears and put on a pair of sunglasses when he bought the phone. He was wise enough to make the purchase at the busiest point on a weekday morning from a clerk who was undoubtedly paying attention to a number of other things at the same time.

My own training in subterfuge and evasion was taught by intelligence agency operatives. I wasn't dressed like any state trooper any of these clerks had ever seen. I was in wrinkled khakis, a pullover shirt with the State Police logo on one breast which was covered by the light jacket I was wearing that did not have a logo on it, but which did hide my pistol, and a pair of Merrell work boots.

Had I been in Michael Ferris' shoes, I would

have come into the store wearing clothes baggy enough to conceal my actual size, either flat soled shoes to look shorter or something like cowboy boots to elevate myself, and I would have leaned just slightly forward to throw off my height when I passed the measuring tape on the door frame. A pair of reading glasses could alter my face as effectively as dark sunglasses without making it seem as if I were hiding behind the glasses. Thick reading glasses would blur my vision and make it difficult to move about the store, but the way those glasses would magnify my eyes could make a sales clerk think I was either blind or someone incredibly book smart. Wetting my hair would darken it slightly and allow me to comb it any way that I might choose. I could grow beard stubble, but not a beard, and shove a cigarette behind one ear to look like one of the greasy bums hanging around outside the store.

Michael Ferris had a three-week head start in our game of hide-and-seek, so he had probably adopted a considerably more elaborate disguise by now. He may have cut or dyed his hair, but it was doubtful that he would have tried to buy a wig to really effect any other major disguise. I did not remember seeing any photos of Michael with facial hair in any of the pictures at his home, so he may have grown a moustache or beard. It occurred to me that I might be better off trying to find the reason why Michael chose to buy the phone from this particular store.

The nearby, but fairly small, Southland Mall would have been a better place to buy the phone and anything else Michael needed to create his disguise. Its parking lot certainly would have been a convenient place to have someone pick him up without being noticed. Michael may have avoided going inside if he thought the Mall security might be watching for him. This was an unlikely consideration because no legal authorities were looking for him at the time. He had been running from whoever sent the men he had killed.

By now he would have understood that the police and his adversaries were both waiting for him to surface. Julie, and maybe his brother, surely let him know that I was hunting for him but that was no reason to believe that he would call or surrender. Despite his having shot two men dead, I was not anticipating another shootout once I found him.

I looked each way at the intersection where the Conoco station was located. The bisecting street ran into residential areas both ways. The street the store faced looked as if there was not much to my right, leaving the narrow commercial corridor near the mall to my left as Ferris' most likely route. A narrow canal separated Main Street as I headed north, back towards Highway 90. I could have driven further into Houma, but I doubted that Michael had gone to ground in any town with such a large police force.

The hunch paid off when I spotted the big yellow and red sign pointing towards a recruiting office for storm-related laborers a few blocks from the filling station. The set-up looked as though it moved around a lot, so it may have been in a storefront closer to the filling station three weeks earlier.

I parked the Cadillac in front of an empty storefront a few doors down and walked to the recruiting office. It would be a tough sell that I was either a real cop or a vagrant in need of a low-paying job if I parked that sedan in front of the place.

The office consisted of two folding tables and

three dozen folding chairs in what was previously some sort of retail store. The wall supports for the clothes racks were still in place and there were no inspirational or advertising posters for the recruiters on the walls, just the one big recruiting poster in the front window.

I took one of the pull-down paper numbers from a dispenser, number forty-two, and zipped up my jacket before I took a seat in the nearest metal folding chair. There were a dozen applicants ahead of me, each one needing barely five minutes to hear the spiel before deciding whether to show up wherever they needed or to reject the idea of working so hard for the pay being offered.

I shuffled towards the right-hand table when my number was called. A tired looking woman in her fifties went through the practiced motions of gathering an application and employee packet for me as I approached. I might have been able to take a direct approach with her, flashing my badge and shoving Michael's picture in her face, but I felt an impulse to approach it another way after I stepped into the waiting room.

I had tugged my jacket to be sure that it hid my sidearm and silently pulled the picture of Michael out of my pocket as I sat down. I set it in front of the woman and waited for her to look at it.

"My cousin come through here looking for work last month. You remember him, huh?" I mumbled and slouched as best I could. I wasn't overdressed for the role of Michael Ferris' shiftless cousin. I figured she was more comfortable talking to that sort of applicant than she would be with a detective from the state police. It occurred to me that Michael would not have risked using his real name to apply, but before I could think what name he might have used, the woman took the picture and gave it a more studied look than I would have given her credit for, before she walked over and asked the other woman.

"I'm sorry, but neither of us remembers seeing your cousin. We see a lot of people here every day," she apologized when she returned. "Are you looking for work as well?"

"I'm a good scuba diver," I persisted in wasting her time.

The woman looked through her job offerings but came back to me with a frown. "There were a couple of companies looking for divers quite a while back, but I guess all those jobs were filled."

"What kind of work was that? Were they good jobs?"

"They mostly involved getting boats out of the way. A lot of boats sank after the storm and FEMA was paying a pretty penny to get the channels cleared so people could get back to work. The jobs paid something like twenty dollars an hour in cash daily and some of the companies even had trailers set up if people needed a place to stay."

"Oh, yeah, I would a need a place to stay. Mama would not like me coming home smelling like swamp water," I nodded vigorously. It was no lie. My mother would never have allowed me in the house after a day of doing manual labor for pay. "Do you have the name of any of those companies? Maybe somebody quit and they still got jobs."

"Let me look," the woman sighed and rummaged through a file box next to her. "Here is a list of the companies we filled positions for. You be sure to tell them who sent you if you get hired."

"Yes, ma'am, thank you," I said and gathered up

the list.

The list of companies spanned six parishes that faced the Gulf of Mexico, nearly half the width of the state. I eliminated the ones past Terrebonne as being too far west. This made my day's decision between a run to Grand Isle, which would be the closest, or to Venice. Grand Isle seemed more likely to pay off, because of its sizeable marina and close proximity to Barataria Bay. I recalled that the charter boat captain had recommended looking there.

My faith in this theory was restored as I read the list. These companies were the perfect place to hide. Michael could work among people that did not know one another, but who would instinctively cover for each other if someone came looking for any one of them.

There were only a couple of companies on the list in Grand Isle that the nice lady handed me, and it was a very small place to search. It was also literally the end of the line for anyone hiding there, as the single highway onto the barrier island ends in the Gulf of Mexico. I backtracked on US 90 to Raceland and headed south on Louisiana State Highway 1. The narrow two-lane road lacked any shoulder as it clung to the banks of Bayou Lafourche and weaved through the vast wetlands leading to Port Fouchon and Grand Isle.

Port Fouchon is a speck of a town on the shore of the Gulf that almost nobody had ever heard of, and that most who knew about it ignored, until Hurricane Katrina roared through and educated the entire world on what a massive percentage of our nation's oil passes through the place. A brand new, and well-elevated, four lane highway linking the port to higher ground was already under construction in anticipation of the next big storm.

It took nearly an hour to reach Port Fouchon and then another ten minutes before I crossed the bridge to enter Grand Isle. There were a few shrimp boats tied up on the north end of the island, but far fewer pleasure craft and charter fishing boats than I remembered being there. At least a quarter of the houses were still boarded up and waiting for repairs from Katrina's wrath. The owners of these weekend camps were most likely still trying to put their homes in town back together. It was going to be a while before anyone had time for a vacation.

I drove past the first Grand Isle address on my list without stopping. It was obvious that the salvage operation was gone and not coming back. There was already a For Rent sign on the window. Unlike New Orleans, none of the buildings here had waterlines marked on them by weeks of standing water. The surge that had flowed across here did its damage and rolled back out to sea in a matter of hours. The only thing that showed its depth were where the lowest boards had been ripped off the camps precariously perched atop piers made of stacked concrete blocks or telephone poles atop footings buried thirty feet deep in the sand. People have occupied this island since the 1780s and knowing how to rebuild homes and lives were skills handed down from generation to generation.

The second operation was located on the lee side of the island, facing into Barataria Bay. A lot of what had been on Grand Isle before the storm had been washed into the bay and this company seemed intent on bringing as much of it as they could find back ashore. A handful of Grand Island's thousand or so inhabitants were picking through that day's haul for anything they could claim or buy. I didn't have a lot of faith in this being the sort of operation that Michael Ferris would have chosen as his hiding place, if only because of this daily foot traffic.

A twenty-something woman, with sun-bleached blonde hair tucked under a bandana and tanned legs sticking out of a pair of cut-off shorts peeking out from under the oversized T-shirt she wore, spotted me as being someone in search of something other than what was currently being offered. She approached me with a mix of island friendliness and a locals' distrust of mainlanders. Her calculation that I wasn't going to make her any money and maybe even cause her some sort of trouble showed on her face.

"Anything special you're looking for, mister?"

"Got a minute?" I quickly flashed my badge. "I'm looking for a guy."

"Who are you after?" she asked as though this were a common event in her day. She certainly had better things to do than serve as the island's census taker.

"This guy," was all I said and handed her the photograph.

She studied it for a minute, moving it in the light to reduce the glare.

"He could be here for all I know," she shrugged. "What makes you think he's here?

"I think he's working as a salvage diver."

"A lot of guys look like him around here," she said shrugged. "Has he got a name?"

"Yeah," I returned the shrug. "But I doubt he would have used it with a warrant out for his arrest. These guys never make it that easy."

"Try me," she said.

"Michael Ferris," I told her. She looked at the picture one more time.

"I know three Michaels that got here since the storm. I know we didn't hire him. There's a big salvage operation over by the high school. Do you want me to call over and see if he is there?"

"No, no," I waved my hands to discourage the thought. I did not want to alert him if he was there.

"Okay," she agreed indifferently. She started to walk away but then turned and asked one more question. "What did this one do?"

"You have a lot of inquiries about guys named Michael, do you?" I asked with a smile, but without answering her question.

"You're not the first one to ask me about somebody named Michael. Just the cutest," she said with something like a laugh and walked away before I could ask her to clarify what she meant by the first part of that comment.

I struck out with the third possible outfit. They told me that FEMA stopped paying for the sort of salvage work I was talking about within a few months of the storm. They had only meant to open the navigation channels, not to salvage every boat and put everyone back to work. It was up to the insurance companies to pay to refloat the last boats.

Leaving Grand Isle at five meant hitting the tail-end of what amounted to rush hour in New Orleans. It was a far cry from the traffic I remembered from the last time I made the drive home from the airport before Katrina. There weren't nearly as many people living in New Orleans now, and there were certainly far fewer people driving home from jobs in Metairie and Kenner than there had been then as well.

11

A GUY NAMED TODD WATERS turned out to be the Special-Agent-In-Charge of the ATF's office in New Orleans. I learned this by reading the metal plate on his door and on the business cards in the handy holder on the corner of his desk. He was a few years older than me, probably a career agent. He was in good shape for a desk jockey. He had a very angular face, closely cropped dark hair, and clean-shaven cheeks and lips that lacked any laugh lines. I was dressed in a pair of dark slacks, an Oxford dress shirt with no tie, and a Brooks Brothers blazer for the meeting. My state police detective shield hung over my belt. Know your audience, as my uncle's tailor had once advised me.

"Detective Holland, what brings you by this morning?" Walters asked with a cheerful and smiling way about him as he sat down in his high-backed leather chair. My dealings with the ATF to this point involved applying for Class 3 licenses for the lethal cache of automatic and suppressed weapons I still owned from my previous career, where weapons of this sort saw more use. I was sure that somewhere in this office there was an active watch-list with my name on it because of this arsenal.

"Well, I was hoping we might work together on

the Grassy Knoll Gun Club case," I tried to make the best use of the limited information I had.

"Those requests usually come from somewhere higher on your chain of command than you stand." So much for his cheerful and smiling phase. He clearly viewed my being in his office as a breach of established protocol, and that seemed to carry more importance in his world than what I hoped to discuss.

"You'll find that I'm kind of special," I tried to keep things polite rather than take my turn in what now felt like a pissing contest. "I report to NOPD's Chief of Detectives despite being a state police inspector. Chief Avery has encouraged me to form my own alliances."

"I'm aware of your situation with Chief Avery. What sort of cooperation are you looking for from us?" Walters asked, but he looked no more inclined to want to work with me.

"I need to know more about the two men Michael Ferris killed at the Beauvoirs' nightclub in the Quarter." It didn't seem like a lot to share with me. The *Times-Picayune* had written an entire paragraph about the two men in the newspaper article on the shooting which Avery thought to include in the files he gave me. Someone had given that information to the reporter, and Avery was noted for being tight lipped.

"And what can you offer me in exchange? You're asking for access to years of our hard work."

"I will deliver Michael Ferris to you. I think he knows more about how pistols stolen out west wound up here than anyone gives him credit for," I gave it my best shot. I had little to bargain with, and Walters wasn't going to be bluffed.

"But you don't have him in hand, and you don't know for certain that he will cooperate with us if and when you finally catch him," Walters threw my lone bargaining chip's lack of value back in my face. "*We* stand a better chance of catching him."

"Are you looking for him?" ATF agents might have been who the girl in Grand Isle had referred to the day before.

"Not at all, but we still stand a better chance of finding him than a state police detective working alone," Walters smirked. Smugness is something I hate, and I would remember this exchange.

"Unsupervised, not alone," I corrected him. "Then I guess you don't have anything to share about who stole the guns in the first place."

"Our concern is that the group behind the gun thefts might be trying to set up shop here. Feel free to keep us in the loop if anything comes up that you think we should know about but kindly avoid doing anything but rounding up your lost suspect." Walters went back to hiding behind his bureaucrat's smile and saw me out the door.

I came away from the meeting with less than I hoped to get, but more than Walters thought he gave me. I now knew that the ATF showed almost no interest in Michael Ferris because they were more concerned about the threat a bunch of illicit gun runners posed to a disproportionately violent city with no gun stores of its own. I'd also learned that Walters was going to sit on the ATF's assets and databases and share what he had only if he saw doing so would be paid back in the form of IOUs issued at the highest levels of any department they partnered with.

I walked away from our discouraging meeting

with nothing new, but I had also palmed four of the supervising agent's business cards that I intended to use as I saw fit.

12

I MIGHT HAVE HAD AN EASIER TIME explaining my problems with arresting Michael Ferris to Chief Avery had I described these reservations in terms of my growing sense that Michael was a very small cog in a much larger machine. He wasn't even a cog. He was more like sand in an invisible machine, and his presence had made the machine malfunction and to become visible to the naked eye. Finding Michael at all was now less of a priority than was being the first to find him. One other party was clearly as interested in locating Michael as I was, or they wouldn't have sent men to get their gun back at the nightclub, or to be trying to lure him out of hiding by menacing his fiancée. I decided that the best way to see who was running the machine was to add more sand.

The ATF was not inclined to help me, but that wasn't my only option for help in bringing chaos to the existing order. I drove to Baton Rouge and parked my shiny black Cadillac among the white Dodge patrol cars lined up in the parking lot. Two uniformed patrol officers started to say something as I approached the building, but they spotted the detective badge hanging from the belt on my slacks. It was a little embarrassing that I had to ask another detective where Captain Kenneth Hammond's office was after I entered the state police headquarters. Contact with my superseding supervisor was usually done over the phone or via messages relayed to me through Chief Avery.

Hammond hated very few things in life, but New Orleans and me, personally, occupied the top of that list. He had worked his way up to his current position from an entry-level trooper, so he was quite vocal about my graduating the State Police academy at the rank of Inspector 2 the day I reported to his office for assignment. He might have made more of a ruckus were I not headed to a city he despised so much. Coming to him for help on my case was an even larger crapshoot than going to the ATF, which I had every reason to believe should have shown at least some interest in a source who could shed light on a case involving stolen handguns.

"I'll buy you lunch anywhere you like I if you are here to resign," Hammond blurted out the moment he saw me. We both accepted that I was going to be a thorn in his side, but he knew that I would never use my family's political connections which put the gold badge on my belt to get him fired or demoted for hating me. It was as close to détente as we could get.

"No, but why I *am* here might cost you a lobster supper." I risked overselling what I had in mind, but it did at least get his attention for the moment.

Hammond closed the door to his office and sat down behind his desk. Hammond likes sitting behind a desk less than I do. He started as a patrol officer and earned every promotion he ever received, only to realize he was working his way further and further away from what he really enjoyed about being a member of the state police. He misses cruising the highway alone and getting to handcuff bad guys. He is physically robust, maintains his marksmanship rating, and sees to it that the detectives under his command produce cases worthy of his praise. I undoubtedly would have benefited from working under him, but we are both just as happy I would never have that chance.

"What might that be?" Hammond asked once he was settled behind his desk. He liked to use his desk as a means of emphasizing his rank over me.

"NOPD has me tracking down Michael Ferris, if that name rings a bell."

"He shot a couple of guys with a stolen gun and the State Attorney's office didn't figure that out until after they released him," Hammond demonstrated his knowledge of the case. I had forgotten that any APB for Ferris' arrest crossed Hammond's desk.

"Anyway, I'm starting to worry that my catching him is just setting him up for someone to take him out."

"Don't give that any more thought." Hammond waved his hand in the air.

"What, you don't think that's the case?"

"It may well be, but you cannot do your job if you start worrying about things like that. Your job is to arrest a violent fugitive. Someone else will have the job of protecting him once you do that, but it shouldn't be any concern to you while you're looking for him."

"Well, it is," I shrugged. "Worrying about it made me look at the case against him. There are a lot of questions that don't seem to bother anybody, but which may hold a key to what really happened."

"So now you are re-investigating the case as well?" Hammond asked. I was adding fuel to his loathing for me by complicating this simple task. "What sort of questions?"

"How do you suppose one handgun, stolen in Wyoming, ended up being used to kill four people in New Orleans? Two unsolved, and apparently unrelated, homicides in New Orleans are tied to the pistol Michael Ferris used to shoot the men that came looking for him. NOPD isn't trying to pin either of those first two murders on Ferris. Michael's brother owns a string of pay-here car lots that seem to be making a lot of money. I have NOPD looking for cases involving cars that had license plates that didn't match the vehicle the witnesses said they saw. The brothers may have a one-stop shop going for gang members, where they can rent a gun and car for the night."

"We might like a piece of that case," Hammond finally warmed to my visit. "What do you need from me?"

"Can you spot check a few of the brother's trailers? It strikes me as a good way to move all sorts of things besides vehicles. That's a lot of trunks," I tried my best to plant a seed that would grow into a burning interest on his part.

"Sure, we can do that. We should be doing it anyway," Hammond wrote himself a note. "Anything else? I wouldn't want you to leave and have to come back."

That wasn't his problem with my visit.

"Do we have anything on the two guys my fugitive shot? ATF isn't being very cooperative," I tossed this out without expecting much of anything.

"The ATF is trying to catch a bunch of idiots who have been trading stolen weapons at those damn gun shows you see at the convention center every month.

The ATF has focused its efforts on tying that gang to Michael Ferris after the shooting, but you're right that it doesn't seem that there is anything to connect the men he killed to the local gangbangers killed with the same pistol. The ATF hopes Michael confesses to something when you catch him," Hammond was a surprising fountain of information. "But first you'll need to catch the guy. Start worrying about that instead of what happens next. That is never going to be your problem, Detective."

"Ah, you called me Detective," I almost blushed, but I was laughing too hard.

"Get out of here," Hammond grinned and waved me away. "I'll let you know if we find anything stashed in the brother's cars. Don't expect a call, though."

13

I ARRIVED BACK IN TOWN with enough time to lift weights and swim a mile at the Athletic Club in the Quarter. The schedule I was keeping in my search for Michael Ferris threw me off my normal routine and it had been days since I had taken time to exercise.

I called Tony to let him know I was on my way home and would like to sit down with him to learn what he discovered in his time alone with Brett and Janelle Beauvoir. He informed me that he was cooking supper for my mother and Tulip so I should hurry if I wanted a place at the table. The alternative was going to be take-out, so I decided to see how the Cadillac ran at high speeds once I passed the NASA Center at Michoud.

The stretch of US Highway 90 between Michoud and the Mississippi border had once been the only way into New Orleans from Mississippi. There were very few reminders of those days left. Weekend camps, perched on low pilings, had lined the narrow strip of pavement winding through the wetlands between Lake Catherine and Lake Borgne when I was ten and my father would drive the family to the weekend house. Most of them were still there the last time I saw my father before Katrina. He and my mother were living apart at the time, and we went to one of the cinder-block diners backed up to the lake for a day's-catch fried seafood platter. It was a ritual from when my sister and I were young and the house my mother now calls home was just a place to go on the weekend.

The storm surge that devastated our family's place had also scoured the lakeshores of most of the other camps and left a full-sized refrigerator twenty feet high in a tree as a testament to nature's fury and the insignificance of any control man believes he has over nature. My mother now chooses to drive to town by way of Irish Bayou rather than see this empty tableau.

I wasn't blind to any of this, but for these few moments I chose to see the loss in terms of how it reduced traffic on the narrow highway. I sped over one hundred miles an hour on the straightaway portions and was smitten with the sedan's grip and handling on the barely banked curves at high speeds.

I parked the Cadillac beside the boathouse and walked to the main house. I walked in as Tony began to hand-whisk heavy cream for the mousseline sauce that he used to top the fresh redfish filets he had gently poached in a copper sauté pan on the massive Viking gas range. My mother never cooked, but she wanted her visitors to envy her gourmet kitchen.

"We were afraid you weren't going to make it in time," my sister greeted me. Tulip speared one of the mussels Tony had simmered in a sauce of tomatoes and wine and held it up to me. I leaned over the counter where she was sitting to eat it.

"I think I have found a place for us to be," Tony said when I stepped closer to him. He smacked the back of my hand when I reached for the spatula beside the pan of fish.

"Do I need Tulip to interpret for you?" I asked him and nodded towards my sister, who was focusing on the appetizers before her instead of the two of us. She understands his broken English better than I do his Sicilian dialect Italian at times.

"A building for the restaurant," he clarified.

"When did you have time to find a building? You're stuck out here unless I or Tulip give you a ride into town. Don't tell me my mother has suddenly decided to get involved."

"The people you had me talk to, they want out of their lease," he said and gave me a big grin.

"Really." I sounded a lot more interested than I was. It was going to look bad if the shooting in their nightclub was behind this decision. My catching Michael Ferris was supposed to encourage them to stay in town.

"They are losing money and want to move home."

"I thought New Orleans was their home."

"Beauvoir is not even their real name. That is Dixon. They moved from New Jersey after the storm because they thought they could fix the city. I was going to kill them both if the husband told me one more time that his family owned a big nightclub in New Jersey twenty years ago."

"It's a common mistake people make, Tony. We aren't like anyplace else on the planet." I had heard variations on this story before. Carpetbaggers have never understood that New Orleans is not at all interchangeable with any other place.

The city's long-time residents were still grappling with the reality that they were not living in pre-Katrina New Orleans. There had been a brief moment in the wake of the storm when the old order was disrupted and doing business here did not require having local connections to get anything approved, but nearly three hundred years of institutional memory of the inequitable way things were always done had proven to be stronger than anyone's fresh ideas or the mayor's good intentions about pushing the city in a more progressive direction. The Dixons didn't understand that changing their names and trying to impose the lessons they learned in far different eras and places weren't going to overcome the problems our local music clubs faced. There was a shortage of local musicians, and the population was unable to support every club in the smaller, but more expensive, city.

"I will remember this," Tony said and finished combining the peaks of whipped cream with the rest of the sauce ingredients before setting it aside and plating the fish filets on beds of freshly made linguini. He spooned a little sauce over each serving and had me help him move the plates to the dining room table.

"Did Tony tell you about the building?" Tulip asked as she reached for her fork. She seemed excited at the prospect of my friend finally starting the business on which she had based his visa application.

"Some. What do you have to do with this?" Perhaps the only thing I was less enthusiastic about than my mother putting her nose in the restaurant Tony wanted to open was my sister getting involved.

"Their lease was handled through an attorney and the building is owned by a shell corporation. I need to figure out who owns the shell corporation so you can make an offer to buy the building."

"Why am I buying the building?"

"Not you personally. You and Tony as partners."

"When did I become his business partner?" I had no recollection of making any such partnership agreement, unless the two of them ran it past me when I was still in my coma or on the morphine drip. I much preferred that Tony and I live entirely separate lives with unrelated sources of income.

"When it became easier for you to get the liquor licenses than a foreign national," Tulip sighed, as though this were something I should have known all along. "Tony needs your name on the liquor licenses, but he is still footing the bill for everything."

"That's good to know," I had to laugh. I had no idea how much money Tony had to invest, but I suspected its source. Millions of dollars went missing at the end of our operation in Iraq. It was why we were being sought for questioning by the Iraqi authorities, and it was also a large part of why I wanted to keep some distance between us.

"Tell us about your case," my mother said to change the subject. Tulip and I grew up listening to the details of my father's cases over supper. My mother wanted us to know what our father did for a living, but she always seemed to view his work as some sort of parlor game the family could play together at mealtimes.

"I'm convinced the guy I am looking for is working as a diver somewhere close to New Orleans. He uses a burner phone to make calls to intimidate witnesses, but he is apparently only able to get to town on Sunday to scare them in person. Friends of the men he shot have his house staked out, but the ATF is acting like he is a smaller fish than that would seem to indicate. His brother owns a string of used car lots, and I asked Avery to review any cases that involved cars with plates that did not match the cars they were on. He could be running a crooked car rental service. I spoke with Captain Hammond about shaking the brother's tree to see if anything drops that connects him to what Michael is involved in. His business moves a lot of cars around and it makes sense that he could use those vehicles to move contraband." I gave my two-minute summation. Tony gave me the same nod he gave in almost every pre-mission briefing. It is a combination of a head roll and shrugged shoulders. Tulip replayed what I laid out in her mind and looked for holes in my logic and conclusions. It would take her a while to offer any opinions.

My mother wasted no time. "What aren't you telling us?"

"Nothing. There isn't a lot to tell at this point."

"There is always a small detail that gets left out," she insisted. "Maybe something to do with your working alone on this?"

"What would your psychic say about my doing that?" I tried to deflect the question the only way I knew how.

"I'm asking you, not him."

"Fine. I'm not very interested in finding the guy I'm looking for. I think doing so will likely get him killed," I blurted out.

"Like I said, small details," she smirked and took another bite of fish.

14

THE PHONE IN THE KITHEN RANG shortly after ten o'clock, just as Tony cleared the dessert plates from which we'd devoured the tiramisu he'd spent the afternoon assembling and Tulip had refilled her cup from a fresh brewed pot of Community-brand chicory coffee. I passed on the coffee because I needed a good night's sleep.

Chief Avery didn't sound very happy. "I've been trying to reach you. I figured you must be out at your mama's place."

"Yeah. I was in Baton Rouge and Grand Isle this afternoon. I got home just in time for dinner. Do you want to know what Tony cooked?" This was my usual cruel taunt. There was damn little that Tony cooked that Chief Avery's heart doctors wanted him anywhere near.

"I'm almost afraid to ask how your search for Michael Ferris is going."

"It's moving forward." I gave no details.

"It was moving forward when I gave it to you. What were you doing in Baton Rouge anyway?" Avery asked me but changed the subject because none of this was what he was calling about. "Never mind all that. I don't suppose you've been watching the local news this evening."

"No." I suddenly wished that I had been.

"Well your stupid antics seem to have paid off," Avery said in a tone that sounded more amused than disapproving. "We arrested a couple of Black kids about an hour ago after they killed two men from Texas near Michael Ferris's place."

"Anyone we know get hurt?" I wondered.

"I doubt you knew either of the men killed on the scene, though you may have recently met them. They were living in a van down the street from Ferris' place. One of them had an infected leg wound. I'm thinking that he might be the third gunman from the original shooting incident." Avery grumbled a bit. He hated messy crime scenes and the messy cases they cause. "I am calling to tell you that the FBI arrested Julie Hart."

"Whatever for?"

"Seems she heard all of the shooting and came storming out of her place with a .357 Magnum just as the uniformed officers arrived on the scene. She started shouting at a couple of other gang members she claimed had been walking by her place all day. Two patrolmen disarmed her when they went over to tell her to shut up."

"And?" This wasn't in my plan.

"The FBI was on the scene and arrested her. They said her actions were a racist hate crime. For the record, the guns we found in her house were not on the list of guns stolen from the gun shop her boyfriend's gun came from. My bet is that they were bought legally," Avery said to move me past the reaction he anticipated I would have to the charges being lodged against Julie Hart. "Oh, my guys didn't find the boyfriend's dive bag when they searched the place. Hers was there, but not Michael's. You seem to have guessed right."

"Any way to get her out of this nonsense? How healthy is our favor bank?"

"You're already overdrawn at mine. The charges probably won't stick anyway. The FBI might be doing this to encourage Mister Ferris to surrender."

Avery was right on both counts. Asking for the FBI to cut her loose was not the best use of the favors Avery had accumulated. Wasting a favor to get the charges against Julie dropped was senseless when any competent attorney could do so. It was a toss-up whether Michael would even hear about the shooting. Turning himself in to get his fiancée freed would be a stupid move that the same reasonably competent attorney would tell him not to make. Julie was safer in custody anyway.

"What I found interesting was the Black kids' claim that Michael Ferris asked them to keep an eye on the place. What do you think about that?"

"Kids say the darndest things." He obviously wasn't impressed with my gift for recalling 1960s TV tag lines. Avery should have been glad that the kids did not give his homicide detectives my name or description.

"What was that all about?" Tulip asked when I broke the connection.

"They arrested Michael Ferris' girlfriend. There was a shooting down the block, and she went storming out of her house waving a revolver and yelling at some of the Black kids who were there. The dead guys had been staking out Michael Ferris' house and a couple of gangbangers shot up their van."

"When was this?"

"Avery said it was about an hour ago," I said and

instinctively looked down at my watch.

"That neighborhood has gone to hell since the storm," was all my sister had to say on the matter. "How's this going to affect your case?"

"Something must have changed to make the shooters think they couldn't wait," I surmised. Tulip rocked her head as if to she was giving that idea some thought. "Whatever it was probably had nothing to do with Ferris."

"It's the most likely explanation. Is there any work in this for me?"

"Not unless you want to give up civil law for criminal law."

"That's a fine line at best, but civil defendants tend to pay their lawyers." Tulip laughed.

15

I MADE ANOTHER FRUITLESS TRIP to Grand Isle on Thursday and started looking for Ferris in Plaquemines Parish on Friday. Only two of the six companies on the list the recruiter in Houma gave me were still operating in Plaquemines Parish.

I could not call either of the companies to ask if a diver matching Michael Ferris' description worked for them, both because I had no idea what Michael looked like at the moment and because doing so might tip Michael off that I was closing in and send him running again. To be honest, another reason I didn't want to alert Michael Ferris was that I believed I knew where he would likely be at some point on Sunday.

Michael seemed consistent about spending his Sundays terrorizing the Beauvoirs, and each visit had involved an escalation in his tactics. The next leap forward from poisoning a dog is hurting a human. I was afraid that this was going to be the Sunday when Michael crossed that line.

I took a much-needed day off on Saturday and was at the Beauvoir home early on Sunday morning. Chief Avery grudgingly approved overtime for a team of four uniformed officers from nine o'clock that morning until six o'clock that evening. Every incident up to this point in time occurred between those hours.

Nine hours of waiting for something to happen is about the limit of anybody's ability to stay focused. Things would happen very quickly if they happened at all. I needed my backup to be able to leap into action from a standing, not sitting, start.

I stationed the two rookie uniformed officers in the house with Brett and Janelle Beauvoir. I told the couple to make frequent, but brief, appearances in their windows and told the uniformed officers to avoid being seen. Their job was to protect the couple if anyone broke into the house. I positioned the two experienced officers in their squad car at the new Home Depot store on Carrollton to serve as blockers for any car that tried to make a run for the interstate. I wanted to point any potential getaway car towards City Park. The park was still a mess from the storm so there would be few civilians around if there was any gunplay. My job was to be sure that didn't happen, but I have multiple scars which remind me how difficult it can be to allow for every contingency.

I parked the Cadillac CTS in the driveway of an unoccupied house on Hardin Street. Most of the homes in the neighborhood were still being repaired, but this one was an untouched one-story house awaiting complete renovation. The familiar scent of decay and mold wafted out of the open windows. It brought back memories of being able to smell New Orleans from miles away when I first came home.

I took up position on the rear balcony of the second story of the Beauvoirs' home. I could lie close to the house and be out of sight from anyone looking over the fence, and I could leap up and have a complete view of the back and side yard once anyone breached the fence. My car was only a fifteen second dash away, so I figured my trap was as set as it could get.

Janelle brought a sandwich and cold drink to my lair just after noon. The strain of playing bait was taking a toll on her, and I was going to have to apologize long and hard if nothing happened by the end of the stakeout. Luckily the day was clear, and the temperature hovered in the low sixties, which made lying outside rather pleasant. The situation reminded me of too many other times I had laid flat on a balcony or sat hidden in an abandoned building to wait and watch for something to happen. You never get good at it, but eventually you learn ways to fight off the boredom that threatens your readiness when the time comes.

My assumption about Michael Ferris' Sunday schedule paid off just after two o'clock. One of the officers from downstairs radioed that a white Buick had circled the block twice. I carefully canvassed the neighborhood before I parked and recalled seeing no Buicks of any color parked nearby, which didn't necessarily mean this one didn't belong here. It certainly warranted close attention, and I was glad Avery sent me at least one officer who paid as much attention as I did. I told him to let me know if it circled again, and how long it took between each pass.

He guessed that the first circuit had taken about five minutes. That meant the car made a larger circle than just a loop around the Beauvoirs' odd-sized block. Whoever was driving the car might be canvassing the neighborhood as well. It was unlikely they would worry about my car, being parked where it was, even if they looked that far down the driveway.

I was still waiting for an update when I heard noises in the low palmettos at the back of the patio. Someone had climbed over the fence and was trying to make their way as silently as possible through a type of foliage that is never easily muffled. I eased my way to the edge of the balcony and listened for the sound of footsteps on the brick patio. Whoever was there would not likely make a dash straight for the back door if they intended to enter the house. There were any number of other things the trespasser might have in mind to scare the Beauvoirs.

One of those was to pour an accelerant against the back of the house. I could smell the gasoline from where I was. I radioed the officers stationed downstairs what was happening and told them to move the couple to the front of the house, but not to open the front door. It was entirely logical to believe starting a fire at the rear of the house was meant to flush them out of the house. Someone could be waiting outside, or perhaps on the other side of Bayou St. John, to do the couple grave harm once they were exposed.

I peered over the edge of the balcony and saw a tall white male in a baseball cap standing a few feet from the back of the house with a gas can in his hand. I saw no lighter or other means of starting a fire but doing so was clearly their intention. I eased my Glock from my holster and brought it to the edge of the balcony. I slowly rose to my knees and prepared to surprise whoever was down there once they had matches or a lighter in their hand. Tossing gasoline on a house is misdemeanor vandalism. Setting it on fire is felony arson. I needed to let them minimally damage the house to have any leverage when I interrogated them later.

What I did not expect was someone else to start shooting. Three shots rang out from where the trespasser had just cleared the bushes. My suspect dropped the can and turned slightly to see who was shooting at him. It is perhaps the most natural, but least intelligent, reaction one can have to flying bullets.

I don't know if he saw who took the shots, but he wasted no more time before sprinting around the corner of the house and heading for the street. I knew that the elderly couple living on the other side of the fence were not good candidates for having taken pot-shots at my failed arsonist. I could not see who fired the shots myself, but I lacked any justification to return fire and did not have a clear shot through the landscaping anyway.

I silently dashed across the balcony to see if the suspect made it through the side gate. They had not, but only because they were waiting for the suspicious white Buick to pull in front of the house. I heard another pair of shots come from the Buick Regal. The shooter this time was firing from the driver's seat and used only his left hand to hold the pistol.

The driver was another white male. He looked to me to be in his mid-forties, and he seemed very comfortable holding the pistol in his off hand. I heard both rounds strike the bricks on the front of the house, and hoped the shots were meant to cover his partner and not directed at anyone inside the house.

I shouted at the suspect hiding behind the gate, which startled him just enough to make him turn towards the sound of my voice and freeze him in his tracks long enough for me to memorize his face. He was younger and much more excited by what he was doing than the driver. He saw the beam of red laser light that linked my Glock to his chest and sprinted towards the white sedan instead of engaging me in a gunfight.

I waited until he was getting into the car before I fired three rounds through the engine hood of the Buick. The engine gave a most disapproving cough in reaction to this as the driver accelerated. I would have had a difficult time justifying shooting either of the occupants. I could not satisfactorily explain that this was my trained reaction to such situations. I realized at the last second that they weren't there to shoot anyone under my protection, and neither of them ever pointed a gun directly at me. I was mindful of the paperwork and lectures Avery would have given me had I killed either man.

I heard one of the uniformed officers scaling the back fence in pursuit of the mysterious shooter. He waved to me just before he dropped over the fence and gave pursuit on foot. My focus was still on the men in the Buick. I ran through the house and out the front door to get to the Cadillac. I was surprised to cross paths with the uniformed officer as I rounded the corner. He pointed at the suspect he was pursuing. That man was already a block away and crossing the wooden foot bridge spanning Bayou St. John. I had no confidence that the officer would catch this suspect.

My Cadillac CTS was more than an even match with a fifteen-year-old Buick Regal under normal circumstances, but I wasn't chasing this particular one under normal circumstances. It was wounded like a gut-shot moose, and I had no trouble picking up its trail of engine fluids. My shots had destroyed at least one side of the engine. I speculated that one or more of the ten-millimeter hollow-point rounds caused the pistons to stop operating properly, which meant the engine was now running on just three or four cylinders while slowly destroying itself by continuing to force the damaged pistons through their broken cylinders. The engine coughed up a little oil and coolant every time it tried to fire on one of the damaged cylinders.

The pair did what I hoped and elected to try to lose me in the maze of streets within City Park. I radioed the cruiser sitting at Home Depot and they put out a call for additional units to block off the park. It was unlikely that there were anywhere near enough units in the area to seal every exit. Time was all that I had in my favor, and the ever-increasing amount of engine fluids from the suspects' vehicle told me that my pursuit was nearly over.

The marked unit I radioed suddenly appeared in my rear-view mirror but kept its distance behind me. They were content to be my back-up once I told them that the men we were chasing were armed and had fired shots at the first location. We were moving through the park at about sixty miles an hour, which doesn't seem very fast unless you have driven at that speed on unbanked and narrow roads. Stretches of the asphalt were still slick with dried mud and desiccated oak leaves dating to their weeks under floodwaters. Trees and branches that had fallen in the storm had been pulled off the pavement and stacked to form guard rails that I needed to avoid sliding into. I watched the driver of the Buick nearly lose control a number of times.

They were headed for Wisner Boulevard, which

formed the far boundary of the park. Their options were going to be limited when they reached that point because they would have to turn left or right, and they had to know there would be roadblocks waiting for them. Bayou St. John runs parallel to Wisner and there are very few bridges across the water. I caught up to them before they reached Wisner, but I did not try to force them off the road for fear that one or the other of the suspects might start shooting again as they tried to run from the scene.

My opportunity to end the chase came when they reached the T-intersection. The driver hesitated for a moment as he decided which way to turn. I made the decision for him and rammed the Buick's rear bumper to shove them through the intersection. I rammed them again and sent their sedan rolling into the bayou. The patrolmen and I were out of our vehicles by the time the pair managed to escape their sinking getaway car. They took one look at the officers aiming shotguns at them, and at the look in my eyes behind the AR-15 I was holding, before surrendering.

"They're all yours," I said and waved the officers standing beside me towards the wet assailants.

"This wasn't exactly textbook," one of the officers laughed as he walked by. "We may have to start calling you 'Crash' instead of 'Cadillac' if you keep doing things like this."

"The Chief says I get to use Plan B. No, wait, he said I *am* Plan B," I joked back, but it was more of a private joke between myself and Chief Avery. The Chief of Detectives wasn't going laugh about what I had done to the front of his former patrol car. "Did you run their plates?"

"The plates are off a Nissan registered in Nebraska," the older of the two officers reported.

"Let me guess. It was sold to Ferris Wheels Automotive." The officer gave me a shrug and a very surprised look when I suggested such a well-known business was involved. "I have something of a side-bet going on whether the dealership is legitimate."

"Well, you may be right yet. We still need to run the VIN on the car. It could be one of theirs."

"Either of you recognize these two?" I asked them. I didn't recognize either of the suspects from my visit to Ralph Ferris' dealership.

"They have Texas licenses. They could have stayed home to act this stupid," the younger officer opined.

"They have probably done dumb things there as well," I shrugged. "Call me when you get their rap sheets."

"You're not staying?" The younger of the officers was surprised that I wasn't trying to claim the arrest for the State Police. Our pursuit was exciting enough to make the television news and papers.

"My work here is done. You two will probably get a nice citation for taking this pair off the streets," I shook their hands before I walked back to the Cadillac. I didn't need to be the one to arrest the men, and I also didn't want to spend the long hours testifying in court that giving the uniformed officers credit for the arrests foisted off on them.

The Cadillac's grille was cracked, and the front bumper was going to need replaced as well, but the Cadillac started, and the gauges didn't indicate I had done anything that shortened the Cadillac's life expectancy. I'd come to like the beast in the short time I'd driven it, but I understood that Avery would not give me a replacement patrol car if I destroyed this one.

Brett and Janelle Beauvoir were sitting on their front porch with the two rookies when I parked in front of their house. There was no suspect in custody, however. I would have been very impressed had the rookie officer caught the shooter.

"He got away?" I asked the still winded officer that had given pursuit.

"He had a Charger parked over by Cabrini," the officer explained. I glanced across the bayou to the Catholic high school and estimated the pair ran about two hundred yards. I would want to remember this shooting suspect's physical condition if I ever encountered him again.

"What about the men who took shots at us?" Brett asked. I couldn't tell if he was paranoid or trying to embellish what happened to look braver to his wife.

"In custody. But neither of them is named Michael Ferris. It's unlikely they are even related to him," I informed them. Something had begun bothering me as I lay on their porch all morning, and it had become an actual question as I drove back from seeing the two shooters arrested. "Did either of you actually see Michael Ferris try to poison your dog? In fact, have either of you honestly seen him anywhere near this house since he went into hiding?"

"He had to have been here. How else did our dog get poisoned?" Brett demanded. It was his story that I was suddenly challenging.

"The same way your house was nearly set on fire. I think these attacks may have been done by someone who wants you to blame Michael Ferris."

"So someone is faking the phone calls?" Brett argued.

"That probably is Michael. But crank calls are not in the same ballpark with trying to kill your dog or setting your house on fire. I'm beginning to wonder if Michael was calling you to try to warn you about someone else with an interest in shutting down any investigation into what happened at the nightclub," I was thinking aloud now, and realized I needed to stop discussing parts of the case that didn't involve the couple.

"Who would that be?" Janelle asked, but without her husband's defensive tone.

"There are plenty of other people on that list," was all I would tell her. "I'd say your excitement for the day is over. I'll let the officers stay around to collect their full overtime, but I don't think anyone else is coming by to threaten you."

"Well, thank you for being here," Janelle sighed and stood up to give me a hug. Brett and I shook hands, but I could tell that he was still upset that I no longer believed his story about Michael Ferris.

16

I SET MY ALARM to wake up early on Monday morning because I felt it was going to be a busy week, maybe not for me, but certainly for the Ferris brothers. I ate breakfast with Chief Avery to get the ball rolling downhill on Ralph and his criminal empire.

Chief Avery was already aware of what transpired at Brett and Janelle Beauvoirs' residence the day before. He carried the reports from his uniformed officers with him. He greeted me in the parking lot beside the St. Charles Tavern so he could look at the damage I managed to do to his car in barely a week's time. I watched him run his hands over the black and chrome grille and then the damaged front bumper but held my tongue.

"I hope you know a good body guy. Keep in mind that NOPD isn't responsible for damage done to their vehicles by members of the State Police," he informed me once he was finished apologizing to the sedan for leaving it in my irresponsible care.

"I'll take care of it. I'm so glad you mentioned that part of your loaner policy when you gave me the keys," I grumbled. I could afford to pay for the repairs, but he had just then decided to change our arrangement, and I wasn't happy about it.

"I would have given you a tank if I knew you were going to use it as a battering ram," Avery shot back, but he was laughing and we let the matter drop.

I followed him inside and we sat at his favorite table by the front window. A different waitress was on duty, but she knew to bring black coffee for Avery and an RC Cola for me. Avery ordered his usual etouffee omelet, but I ordered the chicken and andouille hash I'd spotted on the menu the last time we ate there.

"Have you finished your report?" Avery asked as he stacked the ones from his own officers beside his left elbow.

"No. I don't have anything to add to what your four officers reported," I said and gave something of a shrug. He never approved of my reports when I had a partner, saying they were either filled with too much detail or lacked any at all. I found it hard to make cruising nocturnal streets that lacked any streetlights very interesting. He did not want any written record of my interviews related to my search for my father, so usually I had nothing to report.

"That doesn't mean you don't have to write a report. The defense attorney for the pair you pulled out of Bayou St. John will expect to find one in the case file. Two of the officers claim you fired your weapon as well."

"At the car. Your lab will find all three slugs," I pointed out. It turns out that didn't make any difference, and he told me which form I needed to fill out for having fired my sidearm. Now I was really glad I hadn't shot anybody, though perhaps if I had killed the pair then there would be no defense attorney to satisfy.

"I should put you on desk duty until you're cleared for the shooting, but you don't have a desk. Can you promise not to shoot anyone for a while?"

"Not really, but I'll try," I saw no reason to lie. I knew I was reaching a point in my investigation that someone might get shot. I've been shot and intend to never again be the one who takes the bullet.

Miss J personally brought us our food, wearing the pink bedroom slippers she claims don't hurt her feet like sensible kitchen shoes do. The meal filled Avery's mouth and gave him something else to worry about than my shoddy record keeping and failure to adhere to procedure. My hash was a spicy blend of left-over fried chicken, andouille sausage, chopped bell pepper, spicy boiled red potato, and onion that Miss J ran across the grill and topped with cayenne and a pair of fried eggs. It was going to burn a hole in my belly, but that would make room for a much milder lunch. The waitress was smart and brought an immediate refill on my drink.

"What did the pair your guys arrested yesterday have to say for themselves?" I asked, as much to change the subject as to learn what the Texans had been willing to share.

"Nothing. They lawyered up immediately. Not surprisingly they are being represented by Dan Logan. The car they were driving told us a lot, though," Avery teased me by saying this and then stuffing his mouth. I waited patiently for him to swallow the sizeable bite of food. "Ralph Ferris bought the car at an estate sale in Hammond, but the plates we pulled off it were from a 2001 Altima sold to Ferris at an estate auction in Omaha. Normally we might have had a witness who wrote down the number and we'd think they got something wrong when the plate didn't match the make of the car and let it drop."

"Normally?" I detected something in the way he said what he did.

"I did what you suggested, and we found a dozen incidents of a car being used in a chase or shooting that had plates that didn't match up. Two of those shootings involved the gun we recovered at Michael Ferris' shooting," Avery seemed surprised that my idea actually paid off, and I assumed he was going to take credit for it.

"So you can tie a stolen gun to one brother and a suspicious car to the other," I knew what Avery was making of these details in the case, but I was looking for a different explanation. "What if the brother with the gun had nothing to do with his brother's thing?"

"I'd be quite surprised," Avery answered. "What are the odds?"

"What if Michael stole the gun from his brother and the brother sent someone to get it back?" This was my new theory on the shooting. I'd spent Sunday night considering the possibility that Michael's calls to the Beauvoirs were meant to warn them about the threat that Ralph posed to them, not to threaten them himself.

"I could see that. The only thing is, there was nothing connecting Ralph to the guns until we fished those two guys from Texas out of Bayou St. John. We may never know the connection because the ATF gathered up those suspects this morning. Do I need to remind you that none of this has anything to do with what I asked you to do? You just need to find Michael Ferris and let me know where he is." Avery wasn't in a mood to discuss my investigating any part of the case, which had not even existed until I created it.

"I haven't forgotten. It will just be easier to find Michael if I know who, or what, he is hiding from." Avery tried to stare me down about what we both knew was a rubbish excuse, but I have been stared down by people better at it than Avery.

"You really don't see Michael Ferris as a gun dealer?"

"I don't want to," I admitted. "You would think that at least one of the guns you took from his house would have been stolen as well if he were dealing in them."

"They all checked out as being either his or hers. That gal has a serious taste for big guns, did I mention that?" Avery hadn't, but I wasn't surprised.

"Do you have enough to arrest Ralph?" Our debate cost me my appetite, so I pushed my plate to one side. Avery began picking at what remained of my breakfast, focusing on the spicy red potatoes.

"Not really. He could say the car and plates were stolen. The guys that were driving it will swear someone gave it to them, but they don't remember who. That doesn't matter because we'll never see them again now that the ATF has them." My father frequently complained about stolen car cases falling apart from perjury like this when I was just a teenager. Apparently, perjury was still the best defense. "There is no doubt in my mind that Ralph is doing exactly what you're suggesting, but we are a long way from being able to convict him. We'll have to come up with more. Meanwhile, you need to focus on finding baby brother. At least it seems like you have ended the threat against Janelle and Brett Beauvoir."

"I'm on it," I said and tried to laugh. It didn't

come out quite right.

"Well, since you have the money to fix the Cadillac, you should have enough to pay for breakfast," Avery declared and stood up before I even saw him grab his sport coat off the chair next to him. I wasn't going to argue with him over the cost of an omelet.

"One of these days I'll be able to feed you for free."

"How so?" Avery is all about free food.

"Tony plans to buy the building the Beauvoirs are leasing and open that Italian bistro he came here to open," I tipped him off.

"Well he'd better learn some Cajun and Creole to go with all that pasta. That's all I know about restaurants," Avery offered his advice. It was good advice and something I tried to make Tony conscious of every chance I got. He could make the world's best Alfredo, but New Orleans would judge him by his gumbo.

17

I WASN'T AS SURE about the hate crime charges against Julie being dismissed as easily as Avery seemed to think they might be. Someone was trying to pressure her with the threat of time in a federal prison for what amounted to yelling at a bunch of kids to get off her lawn. If they weren't after her, they were definitely trying to send a message to Michael. The message he probably heard was to dig a deeper hole if this was how he was going to be treated when he was captured.

Tulip called to say she found something useful about the leaseholder for the building housing the Beauvoir's nightclub. She couldn't find the name of any officers of the corporation besides their attorney, but she established that the same shell corporation held the deed to every building connected to Ferris Wheels Automotive Group.

The other thing she thought I might find interesting was that the attorney who represented the holding company was the ubiquitous criminal defense attorney Daniel Logan and not a contracts attorney. I thanked her and then asked her to do a title search for any properties solely owned by either of the Ferris brothers. She asked who was picking up the tab for her time just before my cellphone abruptly dropped the call.

I tucked my phone into the inside pocket of my sport coat and checked my weapon with the desk sergeant at the federal building before going through the series of doors to reach the interrogation room where Julie sat handcuffed to a heavy metal table. I was tempted to undo at least one of the cuffs, but she looked so miserable and vulnerable I chose not to surrender what little advantage I had over her.

"How are you holding up?" I moved a sweaty bottle of water to within her reach.

"I haven't been to sleep yet. I didn't eat whatever it was they gave us for breakfast, either."

"You're catching on pretty quick. The food and beds are both a lot nicer where they're taking you," I said, but I knew that she wasn't going to feel any better in a larger and cleaner federal prison holding cell. "Hopefully you'll get a judge that sees the charges for what they are."

"Which is what?"

"Garbage." I sounded sympathetic only because I have practiced doing so. "You're a pawn in a bigger game and the truth is you're safest if you are off the game board. You can't be threatened with anything once they take everything from you."

"That your advice? Just let them lock me up?" Julie wasn't inclined to do so.

"No. My advice is to get any lawyer not named Dan Logan and fight like mad. But fight slowly and use their locking you up to stay safe. What do you think is going to happen if you go home and Michael is still on the run?"

"So you think my only choices are being locked up or telling them where to find Michael?" She was smart, but she was sharper than I anticipated.

"I already know where to find Michael," I tried to bluff. I had it narrowed down, and I even had a few ideas of where to look if he wasn't in the first three places I intended to look. She proved hard to bluff.

"Well tell him our cat is at my aunt's place when you see him. One of us needs to get Larry before she calls animal control." I had to smile at her bravado. "Why did you really come here?"

"I want to know where Michael got the gun he had the night of the shooting."

Julie studied me long and hard and then focused on her hands and the top of the desk, which was scratched and scraped from the hundreds of cuffed hands before hers. I was asking her to give me something for free that she knew she might be able to trade for something when the ATF or FBI questioned her. I hadn't lied to her yet, as far as she knew. I had, in fact, done exactly what I told her I was going to do and taken care of the men who were trying to intimidate her. She was here because of her own actions and not because of mine, and she knew that was an indisputable fact.

"I'm not real sure," she apparently wanted to tell me something but wasn't prepared to make up a story. "I had never seen the gun before he pulled it out of his pants."

"Out of his pants?" A silly image of a bad pun abruptly crossed my mind.

"He wasn't carrying it in a holster. Usually he has a holster for anything he is carrying," she better articulated what she meant. I'd understood all along.

"Michael was in the habit of carrying a gun into bars?"

She knew I was asking her to admit Michael broke the law. "Yeah. He always said that it was the place he was most likely to need one. He was right."

"I can't argue that." I tried to run a number of scenarios through my head that would make sense of what she was telling me. I was largely at a loss, but then I had a sudden thought. "Were you two together the entire time you were at the nightclub? Did he step away to talk to anyone or go to the bathroom, anything like that at all?"

"He did leave me at the bar for about ten minutes. I assumed he went to the bathroom, but that was the only time we weren't together."

"Ten minutes is a long time in the bathroom."

"It's not like I timed him or anything. It may have been longer or shorter." She might have had more to say on the matter, but the door opened, and a pair of ATF agents motioned for me to leave.

"It's our turn," one of them informed me and pointed to the open door. The way he and his partner yanked my chair from under the table made the gesture unnecessary. If I wasn't finished before, I sure was as of that moment. I didn't have much more to work with than I had when I went into the room, but my previous line of work had taught me what one can build by stacking one brick at a time.

I now knew how confident Julie felt that Michael was well hidden. I could not decide if her comment about the cat I had seen no sign of at their house was a coded message for me or for Michael.

What I needed to do was to go back to the Beauvoirs' nightclub to see how many places I could venture into in ten minutes' time, which is how long Michael had to get into trouble the night of the shootings.

18

RALPH FERRIS' WORLD began to collapse while I was interviewing Julie Hart. Captain Hammond called to congratulate me on my tip as I was leaving the federal building on Poydras. The Louisiana State Police had arrested two long-haul truck drivers on narcotics and weapons trafficking charges after doing a cursory search of the trunks on their car carriers at the weigh station in LaPlace.

"They found guns on one and marijuana on the other. I impounded the rigs so we can inspect each car more thoroughly. The drivers probably won't be very useful. They are independent drivers, and they both claim that they were given the loaded trailers by freight brokers at a truck stop in Dallas, Texas."

"Check their logs and see how many of these loads they may have had in the past. I accept their story only about so much. Ferris probably wouldn't trust such valuable cargo to random drivers." I did admire Ferris' attempt to put an airgap between himself and his supplier, though. The freight brokers would likely prove to be fictional and the numbers the truckers called to get the loads had probably already been disconnected. They certainly would be when word of the seizures made the nightly news. "Are you planning on having a big press conference?"

"We're working on it. ATF is on their way here now to look at the guns. The State Attorney's office is getting a court order to seize Ferris' assets. We'll probably raid his dealership and hold our press conference in time for tomorrow evening's news," Hammond was trying to sound very casual about this, which I knew was killing him to do. He didn't want me to show up and get any of the limelight or credit. I was fine with that, but I didn't want him to spook Ralph Ferris in the meantime.

"Can you hold off on seizing his assets until I call you? I am still working on a few things at this end and having Ferris taken down won't be very helpful. I know Chief Avery would really appreciate your cooperation." Making the request sound like it came from Avery instead of me was not likely to improve my odds of getting his cooperation.

"Have him call me when he's ready so we can coordinate this," Hammond sighed. I could imagine Avery's heated reaction to learning Hammond was positioning himself to take all of the credit for breaking the case neither of them knew about until I mentioned the possibility of Ralph being dirty.

I only needed to buy a little time to put my own plan in motion. I was sure Ralph would be frantically looking for his trailers and having two of them vanish was going to make him skittish. My plan had failed to consider that the investigation might lead to freezing Ferris' assets. I was still thinking in tactical instead of legal terms.

The business maneuver I had in mind to help Tony wouldn't work if Ferris's assets were frozen.

19

I DROVE TO MY MOTHER'S HOUSE and picked Tony up under the pretense of taking him to eat supper at Bon Ton Cafe to get a few pointers about local diners. The ruse was for my mother, not for Tony. He knew we were headed to the Beauvoirs' nightclub to take another look around.

Tony and I constructed a criminal enterprise in our own minds that considered everything I knew at that moment in time. Cars were being sent to Ralph Ferris laden with guns and marijuana, but I doubted that they arrived at his dealership with their cargo. Any contraband was probably unloaded elsewhere before the cars arrived at the garage. Tony liked this idea because taking them straight to the dealership meant almost everyone in the shop was aware of what was going on and that was a stupid way to do things.

Ralph didn't strike me as being either stupid or trusting. The contraband would need to be stored somewhere that it would not attract any attention but would still be readily accessible. Ralph probably would not keep anything illegal on the premises of the car dealership, but I was still curious about the overly secured room across from his office. I needed to see if any of the buildings that his shell company owned could accommodate a semi-trailer. I decided to call Tulip to find out while we sipped our cocktails and waited for Janelle's show to start. She had been on stage when the shooting occurred.

"Are there any commercial warehouses on the property lists of Ferris' holding companies you found in or near New Orleans?" I asked once we had the niceties out of the way and I was able to successfully discourage her from joining us at the nightclub. The last thing I wanted was for her to get involved in the shenanigans Tony and I were up to. She read off a list of buildings and told me what she knew of each.

One address fit the description of what we were looking for, the former distribution center for a mattress store. It was located only a few blocks away on Elysian Fields. This made the two floors above the Beauvoirs' nightclub a lot more interesting. Brett and Janelle were the perfect guard dogs because they supposedly had no idea what was stored above them.

Tony looked over my shoulder as I wrote the address of the warehouse on my cocktail napkin. I thanked Tulip again for her help and hung up as our second round of drinks arrived.

The Beauvoirs claimed they had never gone upstairs because their lease only covered the ground floor. That left a lot of space to search, and little time to do it. I also lacked a search warrant or sufficient reasonable cause to get one.

Tony wanted to get a look upstairs for entirely unrelated reasons. He had regaled me with his plans for converting the first two floors of the building into an Italian-Creole bistro during the drive into town. My friend also used that lost time to pitch creating loft-style apartments on the third floor for each of us as a way to secure my help. I told him my ingenious plan to buy this prime piece of French Quarter real estate for a fraction of its value and explained how I had already put my plan in motion.

Brett Beauvoir spotted us and came by to say hello but quickly found a reason to do something backstage. I did not mention the real purpose behind Tony and my attending this mid-week performance. Brett was lucky that we were there because we were a measurable part of the audience that made our way through the curtained entrance to the auditorium. Tony and I took seats at a table near the back of the house so our comings and goings might not be as noticeable.

We sat through Janelle's disappointingly flat rendition of a handful of New Orleans standards, ending with *St. James Infirmary*, and perked up for the first two performances by the burlesque dancers. I left Tony alone at the table as the third one took the stage, and I was surprised to find the lobby bar had become busier than the nightclub. I was glad to see the bartender flirting with a pair of young tourists at the street end of the bar as I sauntered towards the passage behind the bar. I did not want the bartender to know that I planned to investigate the top floors without a search warrant.

I made my way to the stairwell before I started the timer on my wrist watch. I guessed that Michael would have used the stairs as well because the freight elevator would have been heard through the entire building. The second floor was wide open and empty. I pulled the camera from my pocket and took photographs of the empty space before I climbed the stairs to the third floor.

The concrete stairs, likely built to meet one of the fire codes necessary to protect the rows of centuries old buildings from burning one another down, had a coat of dust that showed recent foot traffic. I shuffled my feet to blur my own shoe size and sole tread.

An unpainted wooden wall blocked my progress once I reached the top floor. There was a padlocked metal door in the barricade. The wall stood roughly eight feet tall, the length of the sheets of the unpainted plywood used to build it. The wall was a minimal deterrence to anyone curious enough to climb up and peek over the top. The ceilings on each floor were easily fifteen feet tall. The metal door was a far more serious barrier, but the padlock was basic, and I could have picked it with little effort. I didn't notice the video camera in the corner until it was too late to worry about being caught on tape.

I took a running start and jumped high enough to grab the top of the wall and then pulled myself up to see what was worthy of such protection. I spotted stacks of boxes on metal racks in the middle of the room. They were set well away from the towering windows at the front of the building. I used the flash on the camera to shine enough light on the boxes to read the labels in my pictures. The boxes bore the names and logos of firearms manufacturers. I made a quick estimation that there were a couple of hundred boxes in all.

I was powerless to keep these guns off the street because I had no search warrant, and I certainly wasn't going to be able to get one by showing a judge any of these pictures. Starting a fire crossed my mind, but that would be even harder to explain. Seeing the arsenal underscored the importance of finding Michael and shutting his brother down once and for all. More people were likely to die until I did so. I did the only thing I thought I could do to sow a little fear into whoever responded to my own intrusion and slipped one of ATF Agent Walters' business cards through the hasp on the padlock.

I was able to get back downstairs and slip past the bartender without attracting his attention. I also put a few yards between myself and the door before one of the waitresses came out of the club to place a drink order. I smiled at her as we brushed past each other before I returned to my seat and checked my watch.

"Fifteen minutes," I said to Tony and showed him the stopwatch. Ten minutes was well within Michael Ferris' capacity to get to the third floor and back to Julie's side the night of the shooting. "There's a gun store on the third floor."

"What are we going to do about it?" Tony asked, fully prepared to consider anything I had in mind.

"I left a calling card for whoever owns the guns." I gave him one Todd Walters' business cards and we shared a hearty laugh.

"Do you think this would be a good building for our restaurant?" Tony asked once that moment of levity passed. I was relieved that he was not letting his grand vision for what he could create within these walls blind him to the financial realities of where it was located. The Beauvoirs' business was failing, and they offered nearly naked women. He was going to be selling pasta in a city that loves its rice dishes.

"It's off the usual tourist path, but we're just a block from Frenchman Street. Locals might cross Esplanade for a good meal before heading over there, but it will have to be an incredible meal. The other Italian places in the Quarter are situated to serve tourists, but you'd have to draw locals to make it. I hope you have deep pockets because building that sort of loyal business could take a few years." I had no real idea of what business was like in the Quarter after the storm, but I had listened to owners when I was eating and drinking in their businesses and few of them seemed very happy.

"What would be a good price to pay?" Tony persisted.

"Let me ask Tulip what she thinks. I am working on something that could give you an advantage in any negotiations for the building." A part of me hoped she would say it was a really bad idea and that I would not need to persuade her to help Tony pay a going out of business price for the building. Tulip answered her cellphone on the third ring. There was much less noise in her background than mine.

"I thought you two were having a guys' night out. Tell me you don't think I will come be your wingman," my sister tried to mock me.

"This is a business call. Tony wants to buy the Beauvoirs' nightclub building. What do you imagine is worth?" I asked.

"Between three and four million dollars. Does Tony have that kind of money?" Tulip asked. Her tone suggested she did not believe he did.

"I think we can get it for a lot less," I told her. "Ralph Ferris is about to have financial problems."

"How do you know that?" she demanded.

"I caused them," I said without offering further explanation. "Can you set up a meeting with Ralph and his attorney for tomorrow? And can you draw up a cash sales contract for them to sign?

"Yes, but I can't imagine why they would consider selling the building at a discount." This was her way of asking for more details.

"Just set up the meeting for tomorrow afternoon and I will have Tony call you in the morning to work out his offer," I told her.

"You do that," she said a bit tersely. She knew there was a reason, and probably a bad one, for my not explaining why I was so sure that Ralph Ferris would sell the building to Tony for an amount that she suspected was going to be well under its market value.

I doubted that her mood would improve once Tony explained what we had in mind.

20

TULIP PLACED A CALL to Daniel Logan, the attorney representing Ralph Ferris' multiple shell corporations, and requested a meeting with their principals to discuss a cash offer on one of the buildings in their rental portfolio. Logan was initially ambivalent about arranging a meeting on short notice, but Tulip's constant use of the word 'cash' in her pitch wore him down.

"Okay, you have your meeting. They will be in my office at three o'clock this afternoon," Tulip called to report as Tony and I finished eating breakfast the next morning. "Maybe between then and now you can explain just what you've put me in the middle of."

"You're helping Tony buy his restaurant building," I reminded her rather than answer the question. "We just need you to draw up a sales contract on their Decatur Street property. Tony is buying the building, and my name is not on the contract or deed."

"Nothing suspicious about that at all, she grumbled. "How much is Tony going to pay for the building?"

"Five hundred thousand dollars in cash."

"First off, does he have that much in cash?"

Tulip seemed more interested in the liquid resources our Italian friend had than the low price he offered.

"He says he does." Tony was having an international wire transfer converted to cash at that very moment. I could almost hear the alarms this set off at the Treasury, Customs, and the State Department by his transferring so much money from an offshore account and converting it to cash.

"That will take care of a down payment. How will he pay for the rest of it?"

"Five hundred thousand dollars is the full offer," I insisted. She paused to see if I was joking.

"They'll never take that. The building is worth at least six times that amount."

"It may not be by this afternoon. Also, make it clear in the contract that Tony is buying the building and its contents. Please, just do what I ask, okay?"

"I'm adding pain and suffering to my own bill, just so you know," Tulip said and hung up the phone before I could respond. She believed I was going to pay her, bless her heart.

My second call was to Captain Hammond. He was going to be a lot harder to convince to do what I asked than was my sister had been. He cautiously agreed to speak with the State's Attorney about the timing of the state's seizing Ralph's assets.

Chief Avery was much easier to manipulate. I only had to offer to buy him lunch at Napoleon House.

"You said you had a break in the case," he said before pouncing on his oyster po-boy. It was going to take hours in the gym to burn off the weight these meetings were threatening to pad onto me.

"The State Police searched a pair of trailers full of cars headed to Ralph Ferris' dealership and found drugs and guns stashed in the trunks of some of the vehicles," I informed him to open the conversation.

"That's not the case, the very simple case I might add, that I gave you." Avery was not pleased. Time was ticking away on my deadline to find Michael Ferris, and here I was telling him about spending that time building an unrelated criminal case against the man's brother.

"They are connected. I don't want to drag Michael out of hiding if people still want to kill him. His brother is the real key to what is going on. Trust me."

"I do trust you," Avery said but not in a tone that gave any indication he meant it. "I simply don't understand how or why you've turned a fugitive case into such a production."

"I'm just following the leads as I find them," I tried to console him. He wasn't ready to hear that this was exactly how I had operated in Iraq. One of the things the control agent on my last mission drummed into me was that you can start an avalanche from the top, but you have to start any investigation into its cause from the bottom. "And I need your help developing my next lead."

"What do you need?" This came with a deep sigh.

"I need copies of the freight bills from the two loads Hammond seized yesterday."

"So call your boss and ask for them," Avery said with some exasperation. "You don't need me to get them."

"I do though," I insisted. "And I need you to ask for them, because there is something in it for both of us if you do so."

"This is where you stop being cute and tell me

what the hell is going on." Avery shoved his plate away. There was still food on it, so I knew I had hit a nerve.

"The State Police plan to arrest Ralph Ferris and charge him with trafficking drugs and weapons. They will be on television making an arrest in your own backyard and the optics are going to be that NOPD's detectives had no idea what was going on." I knew how to start a good fight without having to fight it myself. Professional pride was now on the line for both of my bosses.

"And what does getting copies of the freight bills do?"

"First off, it tells Captain Hammond that you know what is going on and that gives you a foot in the door to his case. Secondly, the freight bills will help me find Michael by giving me a weapon to use against the people who want him dead."

"You're not going to tell me what is really going on, are you?" Avery finally realized he was going to leave our meeting knowing less about what was happening in my investigation than he did when he walked in.

"Eventually. It's all part of that Plan B thing you came up with."

"That was meant as a joke. This isn't funny anymore," he complained.

"I could tell you what I'm doing, but then you'd want to kill me," was the best I was going to give him at the moment. "I will see to it that NOPD shares the credit for breaking the case if you get me the paperwork from Captain Hammond."

Chief Avery was mumbling to himself as he left the table without paying. Part of what he said sounded a lot like he would call me when he had the paperwork. I tossed money on the bill but remained seated. Doing my job now depended on other people doing their jobs first.

21

SEWELL CADILLAC CLOSED ITS DOORS a few years after Hurricane Katrina so I was out of luck on having them repair what had once been their car. The last billboards the dealership posted before going out of business were a clever inside joke about their inventory being pressed into service. The sales pitch was that "New Orleans' Finest Drive Sewell Cadillacs." A stranger would assume this meant the finest businessmen and citizens, but the locals rolled on the floor laughing at the way Sewell was able to embrace NOPD stealing their entire inventory.

Tony walked around the sales floor of the dealership in Metairie while I arranged for the repairs to the CTS' front end. I chose this particular dealership because they offered me a loaner car that would save the cost of a rental car.

"I understand that's one of the cars NOPD took from Sewell," the junior salesman assigned to help me with the loaner car process said. It was a polite way of questioning whether I had the resources to afford a Cadillac of my own. He was younger than most of the salesmen, who were used to selling Cadillacs to people their own age. He was far too hip for me, with his hair held in place with gel and an outfit that made me wonder if he had perhaps dressed in the dark.

"Adapt and overcome, that's what they taught me in the Army. Sewell didn't need their inventory as bad as the city needed cars."

"Have you enjoyed driving the CTS?" He chose a good place to start his sales pitch.

"It's a nice sedan. I wouldn't say it has the sort of oomph I need in a police car, though." The car handled well and could get up to a good top speed, but it did not have the quick acceleration a good patrol car should have. Not that I was ever going to be manning a speed trap or likely to need to build a head of steam from a standing start.

"Are you committed to a sedan?" I liked the twinkle in the young man's eye. I glanced at Tony and saw the smirk he was trying to keep the salesman from seeing.

I was here to get Avery's loaner repaired and to borrow a loaner car from the dealership until that was accomplished. I was not in the market for a car of my own. I didn't even have a garage or parking space in my own name to park the Cadillac I already drove. Tony and I had time to kill and tormenting a rookie car salesman seemed a good way to waste time before Tony's meeting in Tulip's office.

"Well, no. I don't transport prisoners or a police dog. I guess I am open to about anything you want to show me." I made a show of seriously considering the question. It had occurred to me that I could drive a coupe. For all the times I have anyone in the car with me, I could ride a Harley Davidson motorcycle.

"I'm asking because a customer ordered an XLR coupe but died before they could take possession. I am sure you could get a very good deal on it if you are at all interested in buying a Cadillac of your own."

"I don't suppose I could use the CTS as a trade in?" I asked. It was a joke, but the salesman wasn't entirely sure it was how I meant the question. This was not my car. A number of the cars NOPD took from Sewell wound up in other states with officers who had abandoned their stations after one too many shifts patrolling the devastated city.

"Uhm, no," he quickly dismissed the idea and pressed ahead. "Are you genuinely interested in seeing the car?"

"If you are genuinely interested in showing it to me," I shot back. I wanted to tell him to not waste my time acting like I was wasting his. He was the one who decided to sell me a car when all he had to do was hand me the keys to the loaner demo or used car I was supposed to get.

The young man waved his hand for Tony and me to follow him onto the lot. There was a short row of cars with no stickers or markings on them that I assumed were ones the dealership had prepared for delivery to buyers. They were all a lot shiner and sleeker than the three model-year old sedan I arrived in.

"It would probably be a little unorthodox, but I believe it would satisfy your need for speed," the salesman tried to quip as he led us down the row of cars. He stopped in front of a car I immediately knew would certainly raise my game in giving pursuit.

The 2007 model year Cadillac XLR-V he was gradually twisting my arm to buy had a supercharged v-8 Northstar engine that fed 443 horsepower through its six-speed transmission. The salesman claimed it had a top speed that approached that of the Corvette it shared a lot of engineering with. There were just two seats in the convertible's retractable-top interior, which was less of a problem than the lack of a stable roof for a light bar.

There was a flashing light mounted to the dashboard of the CTS, powered through its cigarette lighter, but I could barely imagine the howling protests Avery and Hammond would make over transferring the light into a vehicle like this and calling it a police car. I was equally certain they absolutely would not want to chip in on the gas it would eat.

Tony and I acted far more unwilling to consider the idea of taking a seat in the coupe than either of us felt. It felt nearly bulletproof because of how high the sill and bodywork were and how low it rode to the ground. It had every bell and whistle Cadillac could fit into it, with a great stereo, information screen and a heads-up display of the instruments. That would be very handy once the car was pushed beyond interstate speed limits, or I gave chase on busy city streets. It would be embarrassing to run out of gas mid-pursuit because I failed to keep tabs on my gas gauge.

"Start it up," the salesman suggested and handed me the key fob that activated the push button start. I may have underestimated how wily this kid was. He had the keys on him the whole time and meant to steer me to this car from the moment he approached me. I felt like a sucker.

That realization and sensation did not, however, stop me from pushing the button and bringing the engine to life. It roared awake and I could almost feel the car breathing like an unleashed cheetah.

"What do you think?' the salesman slyly asked.

"It's terrible," I laughed. Tony and I exchanged looks like two kids stealing candy from a store.

"Like I said, the guy who was going to buy it won't be and the family doesn't want it. You could get a pretty good deal on it before my manager puts it on the showroom floor. If you're really interested."

"What's retail?" I had no idea what the sedan I was driving would have sold for if Sewell had been given the chance to do so.

"Right at a hundred thousand dollars." The salesman gave the price almost as a challenge. This was where any tourists would get off the train.

"Cash discount?" I asked and tried not to show how much I was bluffing. I had far more than that amount of money in a trust fund, but until that very moment I had been thinking about how nice it would be to be able to afford to retire one day.

"I could get you into this for just under ninety thousand if you're serious about paying cash. There is a back order on this model so it would sell at a premium over list if we put it on the sales floor." I couldn't tell if this was malarkey or true. Plenty of performance cars did sell at a premium so it might have been, but then I had to wonder why his manager was willing to lose easy money.

"If he doesn't buy it, I will," Tony declared.

"You're just on a spending spree today, aren't you?" I laughed. He was carrying a briefcase full of cash to buy the building from Ferris. This would be a good consolation prize if our crazy plan fell through.

"Go ahead and take it for a spin. I'll let you two argue over who buys it," the salesman suggested. I think he was imagining a bidding war between best friends. That was never going to happen.

It was only a few blocks to the interstate, and we

made it to the airport and back in a short enough amount of time I didn't tell the salesman how far we drove. He didn't bother looking at the odometer to see how far we drove. He did not bother to check the odometer. Our testosterone-fueled smiles betrayed how much we were going to enjoy our expensive new toy. This was going to be the kid's easiest sale of the year.

"How about a down payment and let me take this as the loaner car for a few days?' I suggested once I parked and led the salesman a few feet from the coupe to talk. I left the car idling and Tony sitting in the passenger seat. It made me look more serious about buying the car. I would have three days to get my check back and cancel any deal.

"I'll talk to my manager," he said and tried not to run to his boss with the good news while I could still see him.

"You're really going to buy this car?" Tony asked when I sat behind the wheel again.

"Well, I figure I can afford it now that I own half of an Italian restaurant," I said and gave him my best Cheshire cat grin.

22

TONY WAS DUE at Tulip's office at one thirty. I reiterated that I could not be part of the meeting and made it clear to both of them that I was not going to have my name on any of the paperwork my sister had drawn up or on the deed to the building. I was not unwilling to help him with the licensing, which I was sure would not be necessary until long after today's business.

Tulip had never seen Tony in one of his bespoke suits. The only roles she saw Tony in were that of my concerned friend or a home chef with impressive cooking skills. He looked even more handsome and professional than he did in casual clothes, and I worried what effect that might have on my sister. She was also going to experience his unleashing a few of his less agreeable interpersonal skills upon Ferris and Dan Logan. I was much more concerned what lasting effect that might have on her than his wardrobe.

I had looked into Daniel Logan since our first meeting. He had made a name for himself in New Orleans' criminal court by his brilliant maneuvering. He was also a post-Katrina carpetbagger. He had arrived from Brooklyn and built his reputation by getting cases dismissed for lack of evidence when it became known that the police evidence lockers flooded while the city was covered by the lake's brackish waters. Firearms rusted beyond the ability to be tested, drugs literally dissolved, and documents became mush in the soup that formed in the basement of the court building.

It was curious that someone running a legitimate automotive business would hire a criminal attorney as their corporate attorney. I suppose people might wonder about the amount of criminal work I was foisting off on Tulip as well, but I saw a difference in our arrangement. Ralph Ferris and Logan, who looked more like an oversized, slick-haired evil cherub than the last time I saw him, arrived moments before the meeting. I was monitoring the meeting through Tulip's computer webcam.

Tulip began her career representing clients who wanted access to our mother's family's connections. Hurricane Katrina gave her a chance to represent policyholders against the large insurance companies trying to get out of honoring their obligations. My sister found she could draw upon not just family connections but also the ability to channel our mother's knife-sharp tongue when it came time to deal with the corporate attorneys. Few of the opposing counsel were prepared for such viciousness from such a sweet-looking Southern belle.

"Alright, we're here," Logan declared when the four of them were seated at the table in her office. The notary Tulip shares with other attorneys in her building came in and quietly took a seat at the end of the table, where they could act like they were ignoring what was going on between the attorneys and their clients.

"And we thank you for coming on such short

notice," Tulip assured the seedy men across from her. I had instructed her to control the pace of the meeting because there were a number of things happening outside of the office neither my sister nor her visitors had any idea were taking place.

Tulip wasn't entirely comfortable with Tony's grossly low-ball offer on the building because she was certain that he and I were not being as forthcoming as she normally required of a client, but if it meant helping Tony put an ice pick into either of the loathsome men in front of her then she was willing to help.

"We are on a tight schedule, so if you'd be kind enough to explain why it was so important that we do this today I would appreciate it." Logan apparently had his own agenda. We were using time his client would have preferred using to find the pair of trailers the state police had impounded.

"I am going to buy one of your buildings," Tony declared. He did not state this as an intent, as a desire, or even as an offer. He wanted it understood by everyone at the table that he was going to own Ralph's building before the meeting was over. Logan immediately realized who was doing the negotiating and focused on Tony instead of Tulip.

"Anything is possible for the right price." Logan flashed the creepy, toothy smile that made him so unpopular in the local legal circles.

"Money is only one currency," Tony declared and set the briefcase on the table. He opened it to show the men that he did indeed have a lot of ready cash.

"And what other forms of payment will you be adding to that pile?" Logan asked. He didn't want anyone to think that he had never seen a briefcase full of cash. "I don't see enough there to buy anything my client owns, except a car or two."

"I did tell my client that his offer was low for properties in the French Quarter," Tulip spoke up. She didn't want anyone to think she was as naïve as her client about local property values. Tony glanced at Tulip but did not show any sign of displeasure that she was speaking against him.

"I believe what I am offering will be sufficient." Tony's lips formed a thin smile as he removed a manila envelope from within the briefcase before moving it aside. He left the case open to show the bundles of crisp new bills in their bank bands, within sight but just out of Ferris' reach.

"As I have stated, this looks more like a down payment," Logan dug in.

"I would like a few moments alone with Mister Ferris. I believe we can reach an agreement easier without our attorneys," Tony said and nodded to Tulip that she should leave. She started to say something but spotted something harden in his expression that convinced her to do as he said.

"I'll hear him out," Ralph told his attorney and the only two people in the room concerned about legalities left. The notary took her cue and followed my sister into the hallway.

Tony quietly removed the color copies of the freight bills that Avery had delivered to me only an hour earlier. You could almost smell the drying ink, but you could also hear a pin drop on Ferris' side of the table once Tony slid the papers across the desk. Ralph went pale for just a moment and then leaned over to whisper to Tony, perhaps in fear their private conversation was being monitored. It was a valid fear because I could still hear them.

"Where did you get these?" Logan demanded. Tony noticed the man's knuckles were white.

"From a state police detective." Tulip would have noticed how much Tony's spoken English abruptly improved. "They found much more than this on your trucks."

It was an oddly well-articulated way of saying what needed said without actually doing so. Ralph Ferris knew what was on the two car-carriers he now realized had not been hijacked or wrecked on some desolate stretch of highway. Any comfort he took in knowing the whereabouts of his lost loads was just as quickly swept aside by knowing who had discovered them, and what that meant.

"So this is blackmail," Ferris snapped.

"It is only blackmail if I can stop what is already happening," Tony countered. "I cannot."

"Then why are we here?" Ferris had begun to worry that this was one of those law enforcement traps where they tell fugitives to be somewhere to collect a prize and then arrest them when they are dumb enough to show up.

"Because I am offering you a way to leave," Tony suggested. The term I had practiced with him was 'escape' not 'leave.' Ralph had absolutely no trouble understanding what Tony was implying.

"I think it *is* time that I leave," Ferris decided. Tony took his hand and held him in place.

"My offer is only good for a few more minutes," Tony said in a tone that made Ralph Ferris as concerned as it did curious.

"Oh, I'm sure you will make a better offer if I don't buy this act of yours," Ferris forced a smile and tried to convince himself Tony was bluffing and that the bills of lading were good fakes. But he didn't know where those trucks were presently located so this was an entirely credible explanation.

"You will not be able to sell your building after three o'clock. I will still buy it, but my attorney says I will have to wait for it to be auctioned, and you will not get any of that money." Tony and I assumed this was the case, but we hadn't discussed the matter with Tulip beforehand. Neither of us wanted to tell her enough to scare her away from helping us.

"What are you saying?" Ralph demanded.

"Everything you own is going to be taken by the state police at three o'clock, and they are going to arrest you." Tony informed him in a tone that made it hard to disbelieve what he was saying.

"So, all of my assets are being frozen?" Ferris wondered aloud. Why he was taking Tony's word for this was a mystery even to Tony, but it indicated who was in control right then. Ferris was beginning to mumble his responses and to stare into an abyss only he could see.

"Yes, but not now," Tony made a production of looking at his watch. He had flubbed another word, I wanted him to say, 'not yet,' but Ralph again had no trouble understanding how temporary this situation was. It was about to become a fact because I had notified Hammond that he should proceed enforcing the court order to freeze Ferris' assets just as soon as I told him that Ralph walked out of Tulip's building.

"And that's why you think I am going to sell my building for next to nothing," Logan huffed. He understood that he needed to strike the best deal he could as fast as he could, and that Tony might still be willing to sweeten the offer despite having the upper hand. "The money is no good if I can't spend it."

Tony and I had anticipated Logan's making this

sort of an argument. Tony reached into his jacket pocket and removed a lumpy envelope. "I have a jet ready to fly to Panama and these keys are to a house there. I will include these in my offer. Maybe now you know why I did not want the lawyers here?"

"Fine. I'll sell," Ralph declared in a tone that showed how anxious he was about getting out of the building and leaving the country before it was too late.

Tony stood up and opened the door to the conference room. Tulip and Logan returned to their seats and Tulip sat patiently while Ferris explained his inexplicable willingness to give away a valuable piece of real estate to his attorney. Logan saw no reason to delay his client's departure.

"I guess we have a deal," Logan sighed and gave Tony an openly hostile glare before pressing his forearms on the heavy wooden tabletop.

Tulip handed out copies of the contract. It was a very short contract since Tony's offer was to buy the building and contents as is with no escrow. Tony didn't worry about any liens or anything else that might be messy because the price he was paying left plenty of money for any surprises. It was Logan who looked up from the contract in surprise.

"Why does your client want to buy the contents?" Logan asked in a mixture of curiosity and concern.

"I am buying the contents on every floor," Tony answered without answering the question.

Tulip sat back and tried to act like she knew what was being said. She had already decided she didn't want to know. Logan's eyes narrowed and he stared at Tony as though doing so might let him read my friend's mind. He would have been deeply alarmed to know what Tony Venzo was thinking about just then. It mostly involved how he would have broken Ralph into a ball of ravaged naked flesh and tears had they been magically transported to a concrete cell in the basement of an obscure building on the outer edges of Baghdad. I suspect that Tony has secretly estimated the breaking point of every person he meets, including me and my family.

"Then all of that is your problem now." Ralph grabbed the pen Tulip offered him and began signing. Completing the paperwork took barely five minutes. There were no handshakes or goodbyes once Tulip's notary presented Logan with his copies of the paperwork and Tony placed the envelope with the keys and flight plan into the briefcase and slid it across the table. Doing so made a horrible scratching sound in the otherwise church-quiet room. Ralph grabbed the briefcase and hurried his attorney out of the room. He had a plane to catch.

"What the hell was that all about?" Tulip demanded once I entered her office and contacted Captain Hammond.

"The state police are about to start seizing Ralph's assets and arrest him for running guns and drugs out of Texas. It's why Tony insisted the notary write the time the transaction was made on the contracts."

"What was in the envelope you gave Ralph?" Tulip asked Tony.

"A plane ticket to Panama and keys to a house," Tony shrugged indifferently.

"You two just helped a suspect flee the country. I could be disbarred." Tulip managed to say without screaming. Her facial expression did that for her.

"He's not fleeing the country," I assured her. "He

is legally considered to be a free man until an arrest warrant has been issued. I asked Hammond to delay the State Attorney's office doing so until we were done."

"What are you going to tell Bill when he finds out what you two have done?"

"He already knows that there is a private jet waiting for Ralph at Lakefront Airport," I answered. "It cost Tony a pretty penny. Ralph will never use the keys because the jet is chartered to fly around the Gulf of Mexico until dark and then to land at a private strip out in Houma. Captain Hammond and Chief Avery will be there to greet him, along with lots of news crews."

"And what was the big drama about buying the contents?"

"Ralph has a stockpile of stolen guns on the top floor. He probably thinks Tony just bought a world of trouble." I reminded Tony that he'd need to call the ATF to come collect them.

"And you decided not to tell me any of this." Tulip's simmering anger was now free to boil over and scald both of us.

"It was a lot to explain in such a short time," I tried to lie. Tulip punched my chest. It's her normal target because she claims I'm too handsome to slap. She's probably more worried about hurting her hand on one of the plates covering the rebuilt face she picked out of a magazine.

She and I both knew how unlikely she would have been to agree to be part of this voluntarily. She could now honestly testify that all she was hired to do was handle the real estate transfer contract if Tony's purchase of the building were ever challenged in court. My name was nowhere to be found on any of the paperwork and Tulip knew better than to volunteer anything that might incriminate herself or a client.

"I guess this is more pain and suffering you can add to your bill," I laughed and scurried out her door behind Tony before she could throw anything.

23

TODD WATERS WAS not amused to find his business card in the padlock after Tony called to have him seize the weapons he claimed to have found while inspecting his new property. At least Waters didn't cry about looking like a fool, as Ralph Ferris had done when his jet to Panama made an unexpected landing, and Hammond and Avery jointly paraded him before the news crews in handcuffs and displayed his half a million dollars in cash to feed the insatiable twenty-four-hour news cycle. It was the only warning the Grassy Knoll Gun Club was going to get to expect an ATF raid.

Ralph's arrest was becoming the stuff of legend for the State Police and NOPD officers who took joint credit for breaking the case. Avery called me early the next morning to tell me to meet him at St. Charles Tavern for lunch, saying only that we had things to discuss about the Ferris matter. He did not sound like his intention was to fire me for having expanded a simple manhunt into what it became.

He ordered a fried oyster po-boy and I asked for something called Mary Elaine's meatballs, which proved to be savory meatballs in marinara sauce atop a bed of fettuccine Alfredo. It looked interesting and the mix of flavors proved to be amazing.

"I have been thinking," Avery said to open the one-sided conversation. "You suck at paperwork but have a nose for finding crimes. Captain Hammond and I were talking while we waited for that jet last night and he suggested that I consider using you as a bird dog instead of a retriever.'

"Well, he hates me," I was quick to point out. It came as no surprise that Hammond wanted Avery to think of me as sub-human.

"It's a good thing," Avery chuckled. "I can assign you to look into things that don't look like much on the surface. You would kick over a few stones and ask a few questions to see if there might be more to it than we think. I will assign any investigation to my own detectives if you find anything worth pursuing. It means you don't have to worry about paperwork or ever testifying in court."

"What's the catch?" I asked. It sounded too good, and I got my head cracked open the last time I was asked to work off the books.

"You don't get credit for anything you find," Avery said and visibly tensed as he waited for me to react to the proposition of working in obscurity.

"I'm in," I decided. "I assume this means I do not have to play by the rules, either."

"You can't go off the rails," Avery was quick to set restrictions. "No physical or verbal threats, no beating anybody up, and no killing anyone. Do not do anything that might get reported to internal affairs, because you need to stay behind the curtain."

"I can do that," I shrugged. "Right after I lay hands on Michael Ferris."

"That is over and done with. Let it go," Avery said and took another bite of his sandwich.

"We have a bet. I still plan to win it," I told him.

I was still playing a hunch, but the idea was now more of a conviction than it was an educated guess. Michael enjoyed scuba diving but wasn't experienced enough to do commercial work. Someone tosses a piece of meat into the Beauvoir's backyard that smelled like kerosene to Brett, but it might have smelled like something called Corexit. Michael Ferris seemed to be pretty well known at the dive shop in Westwego. It wasn't too much of a stretch to imagine he was also popular among the local dive boat captains.

"I checked a list of local dive boats and found that a boat captain I spoke with at Temento's is Julie Hart's father. I think Michael is hiding out on the guy's boat, or that he knows where to find Michael."

"I'm convinced, but it doesn't matter. Michael Ferris isn't even wanted as a material witness now that his brother has agreed to testify against the guys from Texas. He even swears Michael had nothing to do with any of his illegal activities. Todd Walters called me this morning and said to leave Michael Ferris alone. Your case is done," he said and reached for his heavily sweetened coffee.

"I'm still going to check it out."

"I just told you not to bother," Avery said, a lot less cheerfully.

"We still have a bet," I reminded him. "And I want to know if I still know how to play a hunch."

"Don't let pride be what drives you. I will stipulate right now that you've found him and buy you dinner if you drop it. The last thing I want to do is get crosswise with the ATF," Avery nearly pleaded. I saw his point and sympathized with his situation.

Avery had signed off on the findings of an internal investigation by his detectives into the shootings on Danziger Bridge in the aftermath of Hurricane Katrina. They had concluded that the two deaths and four injuries had been justified use of deadly force. A federal review of the same evidence came to the opposite conclusion and the officers involved had been indicted in federal court barely two months earlier. Avery was now in hot water with what the FBI was calling a coverup and the new police superintendent seemed prepared to jettison Avery's career to save NOPD from falling under a consent decree. My unnecessarily adding a second federal agency to the of list of agencies calling for Avery's head on a platter was not appreciated.

"You're not the first person to warn me about confusing determination with pride. It nearly cost me my life the last time, and it may cost me a job this time, but I have to know I am right about where he is," I told Avery as I stood up to leave.

I had started my Army career as an analyst in military intelligence. My economics degree program from LSU gave me the skills to locate bad guys. I gave up my air-conditioned office to endure Ranger selection and then passed selection as a Green Beret. I eventually caught the attention of recruiters for the Army's legendary shadowy outfit which refuses to acknowledge its own existence. I honed my skills at targeted death during the five years I worked with the best anti-terrorist warriors on the planet. It all ended when a Black Hawk helicopter I rode in caught a sharp down draft and left me with two broken kneecaps on the side of an Afghan mountain surrounded by men determined to kill me.

The physical therapy following my knee surgery convinced me that returning to the field at less than one hundred percent put everyone else's life at risk.

I took a medical discharge and flew to Baghdad because I was left unprepared for civilian life by the mindset and comfort with extreme violence I still had, but I needed to stay busy.

My military school roommate had recommended me for what proved to be an unsanctioned operation focused on neutralizing the groups behind the IED attacks on Coalition troops. I would select the targets and Iraqis would handle the wet work.

Tony had led this team of killers, and we eventually found ourselves hunting for an insurrectionist group financed with the billions of dollars in currency our Treasury repatriated to the Iraqis. Tony and I worked our way up their chain of command until we were told that the former Iraqi army colonel bankrolling the attacks.

We were warned that he belonged to a family too powerful to cross. We were ordered to leave him alone, but we decided to take him into custody. We were ambushed by men determined to free him, and the rest is history.

You would think that a near-death experience like this would have taught me to follow orders, but I was dead set on locating a man that I knew no longer posed a threat, and that nobody even wanted to see in custody any longer.

24

IT TOOK A LITTLE OVER AN HOUR to drive to Venice. I drove under a sky that made me wonder why all cops don't drive convertibles. Newly paved highway ran as far as Empire, but the final distance was between the levees that separate the Mississippi River from the Gulf of Mexico. The road ended in Venice, which is the southernmost town in the state. It sits one yard above sea level and is nearly within sight of that sea.

I parked the Cadillac so as to block the entrance to the marina's crushed shell parking lot. I checked my Glock to be sure there was a round in the chamber and that the safety was off before I secured it in the thigh holster that I was wearing to show off the fact I was armed. I wore a light-weight nylon jacket with the words State Police emblazoned on the back over the ballistic vest I pulled from the bag of necessities in the trunk in the Cadillac. I wore my badge on a strap around my neck for all to see, but the marina was largely empty.

I started walking down the pier and reading the names of the charter boats. I wasn't there to search every boat, just the one I should have had a search warrant to board. The boat I was looking for was tied off to the dock and on shore power when I located it mid-way down the pier on Tiger Pass Road. The heavy metal cover plates over the diesel motors were open and two men were working on one of them. Captain Hart glanced up and recognized me before he ducked his head back down to what he was doing.

"I need to speak with Michael Ferris," I said and rested one foot on the stern gunwale. It afforded me a view directly into the engine compartment at both men.

"Nobody here by that name," the other man said. He was right. They were both too old.

"That doesn't mean you don't know where he is," I pointed out. The pair looked at one another and then Captain Hart stepped off the boat to speak with me. He busied himself with wiping his hands on a red shop towel and I did a quick threat assessment. He had no knives or tools on his belt or in his hands, and I saw no unnatural bulges under his clothes to indicate he might be armed, which I considered to be unlikely, anyway.

"Are you harassing me just because we met at Temento's?"

I thought that was a novel argument and I smiled at its simplicity.

"I wouldn't say I'm harassing you. You didn't have to stop working on my account. You could have just said you don't know where he is. Now I think you do."

"Are you accusing me of harboring a fugitive? Why would I admit to doing such a thing?"

"Maybe because you think Michael's going to be a pain in the ass as a future son-in-law," I suggested. The captain looked stunned, but I couldn't tell whether I genuinely surprised him by having made the connection to his daughter. "Michael stopped being a fugitive when they arrested his brother last night. He's a material witness at best, or worst."

"A witness to what?" The captain seemed very interested in a man he'd already tried to claim wasn't around.

"I'm working on this theory that he stole a gun he didn't know was already trouble for his brother. See, it turns out that his brother was renting out warehouse space to a bunch of yahoos from Texas. Michael found the stash and likely thought nobody would miss one gun, but these guys were a lot more possessive than he imagined." I saw no harm in telling this stranger what would be in the papers fairly soon. Ralph had tossed anyone he could under the bus when he realized the range of charges he was facing and the amount of prison time each charge carried. Daniel Logan was going to earn his fee.

"So what do you need Michael for if his brother's the one in jail?"

"I need to hear his side of the story," I said.

"I'm pretty sure this Michael guy wouldn't want to get involved any further. Not that I know him or where he is," the captain continued to try to stymie me. We were past establishing his involvement. Now he was doing his best to stall me.

"It's probably best if he tells me that himself," I pointed out. "And then you could get back to what you were doing. How's that sound?"

"Not very good for Michael," the captain said. I was slow to realize he had been looking past me and not at me the whole time. It wasn't apparent until I closed the distance between us as we spoke.

I turned around and caught a fleeting glimpse of a shirtless man running from the deck of a boathouse across the marina.

I turned back around to find the captain was running away from me as well, but he wasn't who I came to see, and I ran for my car instead of going after him. I didn't know if Captain Hart hoped I might follow him, but he was going to be winded for nothing when he finally turned to find I didn't take the bait.

I kept an eye on the boathouse as I dashed to the Cadillac. I hastily counted the number of boathouses between the end of the row and the one I now believed Julie's father allowed Michael to use as a hideout. I also kept an eye between the close-set boathouses for any vehicles speeding away. It was an absurd notion to think you could outrun law enforcement on this road. I only needed to radio ahead to any of the sheriffs or state troopers in the area to stop him somewhere along the sixty miles between here and Belle Chase. Then I remembered I was driving a car with neither a police radio nor a pursuit light bar.

I pulled in front of the boathouse and again used the coupe to block the roadway. I was surprised to find Julie's Chrysler convertible in the driveway. This wrinkle added the probability that Michael Ferris had the help of someone else I hadn't yet encountered, which meant I might have at least two armed men to deal with once I entered the boathouse.

The movies always show cops boldly kicking in the door at times like this, but what normally happens is that the cop with the coolest head tries the doorknob first. Often, such as this time, the door proves to be unlocked. You still have to open the door and risk immediate gunfire.

I opened the door but pressed myself to the right

of the doorframe, out of the line of fire if that was how Michael chose to react. There were so many guns involved in this mess that I had no choice but to assume there was at least one more at his disposal.

I opened the door and was confronted with a screened-in picnic area, designed to let storm surge pass beneath the house, and a flight of stairs leading to a closed door. I was going to be fully exposed the entire way up those stairs. I aimed my pistol and began an adrenaline-fueled climb up the creaking wooden steps. I was inclined to shoot anyone who opened the door. I did not want to shoot Michael Ferris, but I have learned how unpredictable a man can be when he feels cornered.

"Michael Ferris?" I shouted before I reached the top of the staircase. "My name is Cooter Holland. I am a detective with the state police. Can we talk?"

"He knows who you are, Detective Holland. Come on upstairs," Julie Hart shouted through the closed door. I hurried up the stairs as much because I knew it was safe to do so as to find out what the heck was going on.

Julie Hart and Michael Ferris were waiting for me on the sofa when I entered the living room. I had not expected to see her here, but it was the man sitting at the kitchen table that drew my attention. Todd Walters was seated across from another ATF agent. The way everyone in the room looked at me made it clear they had been waiting for me to arrive. I flicked the safety on my pistol before I holstered it.

"Nice to see you again, Miss Hart," I said as I pulled a chair from beneath the table and sat down across from Walters. I turned to him for an explanation. "I can't wait to hear *this* story."

"Michael has been working as an informant for the ATF for almost a year. The night of the shooting, Michael broke into a storeroom above that nightclub to take a gun from the stockpile so we could trace its serial number. As you discovered on your own, the upper floors have security cameras. Whoever was watching the cameras sent three men to kill Michael and recover the pistol. Michael went on the lam when the State Attorney's office decided to press weapons charges before they spoke with us. Julie agreed to tell us where Michael was, but only if she could join him. We asked the FBI to take her into custody after the shooting she says you played a part in making happen and she brought us here. We can discuss that shooting some other time, along with you leaving my business card all over town." Walters was generous with the highlights but made sure to end his disclosures by threating me instead of just asking that I promise to keep his secrets.

"Do you really think your brother sent those men to kill you?" I asked Michael. I'd met Ralph and still couldn't make up my own mind about this.

"I don't know if they were sent to kill me, but I thought they might kill my brother if they didn't get the gun back. I knew he was involved with them."

"What's up with those guys from Texas, anyway? One of them tried to set the Beauvoirs' house on fire last Sunday," I really hoped Walters could offer just a little more insight.

"The government sells its surplus military guns, mostly old .45s and Garand rifles, to registered gun clubs and this bunch bought all the guns they could before someone either looked at the stupid name of the club these guys had formed one more time or counted the number of guns they were given. They sold the guns for a small fortune to collectors and used the proceeds to go on a burglary spree. They hit gun stores in four states. Their leadership have connections to some of the wackier militias and white supremacists. Their intention here was to sell enough guns to Black street gangs and drug dealers that they would kill each other off. Mike's brother had a plan of his own and just needed a source of untraceable guns. He rented the gangs a car he could report as stolen and as many guns as they needed to do their thing. That way they didn't have to worry about having to acquire or dispose of their guns, or stealing a car, and Ralph could keep using the same hardware over and over again. He'd sell the cars, and nobody was ever the wiser because NOPD saw the mismatch in the plate numbers witnesses gave and the cars used and wrote it off to bad vision or bad memory." I was starting to wonder why Walters was suddenly being so generous with the details of what I was sure was a major case he had yet to prosecute.

"My brother wanted me to run that part of his business because he didn't want to have to deal with the nutso guys from Texas. It didn't take me long to realize they were just a bunch of crazy racists, so I turned him down," Michael spoke up. Having seen this Texas clan in action I could understand why both of the Ferris brothers wanted to keep their distance, but Ralph apparently could not bring himself to stay away from the money this sideline generated.

"So, why did you call the Beauvoirs every night and why were the Texans trying so hard to run them out of town?" The answer to these questions was what made the drive to Venice worth the effort. I had a dozen theories and believed that every one of them probably made more sense than the truth would.

"I was calling them to try to get them to leave. Those two were unaware of what was going on over their club, but it was only a matter of time before one of them figured it out and then all hell would have broken loose. The Texans were the ones attacking them. They knew I would be blamed for what they did, and they were counting on somebody like you to drag me out of hiding." Michael's explanation matched the best one that Tony and I had come up with. At least it tied everything together.

"Well, everyone gets their wish. The Beauvoirs decided to move back to New Jersey as fast as they can get packed after the arson attempt on their house." I noticed that my mention of this incident came as no surprise to the ATF agents. "I don't suppose you know anything about the shooter at their house last Sunday?"

"I wouldn't comment either way if I did," Walters snorted.

"For the record, your shooting of those two men was ruled to be self-defense. I think the ATF used the State Attorney's office to get NOPD to assign someone to look for you rather than expose the fact that you were working for them," I said to Michael.

"Which you are not going to do," Walters reminded me. I finally had the answers to all of the questions that continued to bother me, not that knowing everything would ever matter to anyone else.

"I could follow the two of you home," I offered Michael and Julie.

"I think we're going to stay here until things cool off," Michael said, and I watched him squeeze Julie's hand. "The ATF wants to put us in witness protection, but we told them no. I'm not going to leave here just because my brother is a crook."

"Things aren't likely to cool off just because your brother rolled over on the guys from Dallas." I hadn't heard about any arrests in Texas so it looked like their getaway vacation might be indefinite. I stood up and acted as if I was starting to leave but turned to speak with Julie.

"Your dad must be so happy to be part of all this."

"He's cool with it," Julie rebuffed me. "What are you going to do now?"

"Leaving people alone really isn't what I do for a living," I hated to admit.

"No, you certainly seem to enjoy complicating other people's lives," Julie commented. "I was scared to death when those kids started shooting up that van."

"It certainly got the ball rolling." I remained unapologetic for my actions. I took out my cellphone and dialed Avery's telephone number. The couple watched me with considerable apprehension.

"There's someone I need you to talk to," I told Walters and handed him the phone before the Chief of Detectives had time to answer. I moved towards the sofa to speak with the couple while the ATF agent was busy.

"I won't tell my boss where you're hiding. He has already washed his hands of this matter. You two are now the ATF's problem, and they are your problem, so good luck with that." I assured the couple and walked back to take my phone from Walters, who was still laughing about whatever he and Avery had discussed.

"Bill bet me that you wouldn't let this drop. It's

why I thought we should be here to greet you. I guess I owe him for an expensive dinner." Walters said as he returned my phone.

"I'm tenacious." I shrugged. "You might keep that in mind."

All that mattered to me right then was that I had caught the rabbit Avery told me to chase. I was enjoying a feeling I hadn't had since I was forced to leave Iraq and stopped chasing down truly bad men. I knew I could adjust my skill set to meet Avery's need for a civilian shadow warrior.

Walters had no retort to my response. I willed myself to walk away without saying another word. My phone rang as I was getting into the Cadillac. It was Avery, who I assumed had to hang up and collect himself before he could talk to me.

"I could have told you about the ATF, but you still would have gone down there." He sounded like he was in a much better mood than when I had left him.

"Go ahead and laugh. You still owe me that dinner," I told him and hung up.

I drove the whole way back to town imagining ways to run up the tab at K-Paul's now that I knew that the ATF was going to reimburse Avery for the meal.

I also tried to imagine what Avery and Hammond were going to have to say when they learned I was going to use the XLR as a patrol car. I was certain that they were not likely to find the personalized plates I ordered as funny as the sales manager at the dealership did when he wrote down the words 'COP CAR' on the personalized license form.

OTHER BOOKS BY H. MAX HILLER

Cadillac Holland Mysteries
Blue Garou
Can't Stop the Funk
Ghosts and Shadows
Parish the Thought
Everybody Pays
Shell Game

www.ingramcontent.com/pod-product-compliance
Lightning Source LLC
Chambersburg PA
CBHW050143110726
47898CB00008B/2642